W9-ARO-220

For several minutes she lay there, waiting for him to come to bed, but he didn't. She was sure he was still in the room, thought she could hear the faint sound of his breathing. But she couldn't be certain; the radio was still on, masking most of whatever sounds there might be.

Finally, cautiously, she opened one of her lids a crack. The room was dark. Her eye roamed it, and came to a stop near the window. He was seated in the small chair near the sewing machine. He seemed to be facing her.

There was something looming and monstrous about his shadow, something chilling about his complete lack of movement and total quiet. Frances felt her heart begin to race, her breath quicken. She tried to stifle her breathing, afraid he would hear and realize she was awake, was bluffing, but it only seemed to make it worse.

Her lips began to form a word . . . and then stopped. She realized she was too afraid. *I'll lie here and watch him*, she thought, *be ready to run, to defend myself if I have to. . . .*

NEVER TELL HIM YOU'RE ALONE

Richard O'Brien

ST. MARTIN'S PAPERBACKS

NEVER TELL HIM YOU'RE ALONE

Copyright © 1992 by Richard O'Brien.

Cover illustration by Neal McPheeters.

ISBN: 0-312-92826-2

Printed in the United States of America

St. Martin's Paperbacks edition / April 1992

10 9 8 7 6 5 4 3 2 1

To Alison, Charles, Sean,
Rebecca and Julie, with love

Chapter
1

"DO YOU KNOW HOW I FEEL, NOT BEING AFRAID? NOT LOCK-
ing my door every time I leave the house? Not locking
it during the *day*, while I'm inside the house? I mean,
after all, when I've lived practically my whole *life* with
apprehension?"

Frances Sommers was saying all this, spewing it out,
to Mrs. Emenesky. Mrs. Emenesky—Frances had no
idea what her first name was—lived nearly two hundred feet down the road. She was Frances' nearest
neighbor. Like most of the women in this area of New
Jersey, she wore her graying hair in a too-careful-look-
ing bouffant style. A widow in her sixties, maybe early
seventies—Frances couldn't really tell—she was very,
very heavy, and friendly in the way all the people
seemed to be out here. Friendly enough to smile and
say hello. Not friendly enough to engage in long conversations. Certainly not friendly enough to invite you
into their homes.

Frances, having completed her unplanned outburst,
looked uncertainly at Mrs. Emenesky. *Maybe I said
too much, opened myself up too far?* In all the months

she'd lived here, this had been the longest exchange between Frances and any of her neighbors.

The poor woman, Frances thought humorously. *The one time she happens to walk past, I'm out here and collar her.* Mrs. Emenesky rarely walked any farther than to her mailbox and back. Waylaid by Frances, all the aging woman had said to her was a mild, innocuous, "How are you enjoying it here?" After which Frances' rush of words had followed.

If she felt beleaguered, Mrs. Emenesky showed no sign of it. She simply stood there in the early July sun and shook her head, looking a little dazed, but hardly put-upon.

Frances shrugged her shoulders. "But then I guess you've lived here all your life. It must seem odd to you that people even *think* about locking their doors."

Alertness reappeared in Mrs. Emenesky's eyes. "Oh no," she said emphatically. "Mr. Emenesky and I always locked our doors at night."

Frances felt a wave of relief surge through her. *So then it's okay to do that.* A local custom. She'd been afraid it was a vestige, a vestigial trace, of her New York paranoia. *A local custom. Maybe they all do it.* So maybe she wasn't the city-bred coward she'd feared she was. Frances smiled. A breeze that stirred the trees lining the small country road lightly tossed her short blond hair. "I *am* enjóying it here," she said, finally getting around to giving a simple answer to a simple question. "I *love* it," she finished, as emphatic in her way as Mrs. Emenesky had been in hers.

"Well, good. That's good, then. See you again soon, I hope," Mrs. Emenesky nodded. All her chins awaggle, she heaved her bulk about and began to return to her home. Having walked up the road, fruitlessly searching for a lost pet, she had been on her way back when Frances had come upon her.

"If I find your little dog, I'll bring him to you," Frances shouted after her, sincerity mixing with a need to keep the conversation, *any* conversation, going. But Mrs. Emenesky, still moving away as quickly as she could manage, didn't hesitate or turn, simply raised a plump hand in acknowledgment.

Frances allowed herself a wry grin. *It's all right.* She thought back to her hometown. *How different are the people here, really, from the ones back in Brooklyn? All of us there passing each other in the streets, even in our apartment houses, day after day, most of the time never speaking to each other, even after we'd been doing it for years. And the few conversations that did take place—only a few much longer, or more probing, than out here.*

Yet somehow it never felt quite right here. You were *supposed* to be impersonal in the city. This was the country, the sparsely populated, very rural northwest corner of New Jersey. She'd expected more warmth. *Ah well,* Frances thought, glancing back toward the house she loved so much, *don't be greedy. You have warmth enough. Right there.*

A computer date. They laughed at it now, marveled, too, that somehow, incredibly, it had worked. But at the time, she hadn't laughed, had felt humiliated to find herself doing something she'd promised herself she never would. And yet . . . because of that date, there was Jeff, standing by the window, grinning out at her, holding David, their wonderful, terribly bright and loving son.

Ten years out of college, she'd been on her own too long, had taken a last, desperate stab—and it had worked out. She smiled back and waved, then finally completed the task she'd come out here for. She walked across the narrow asphalt road to their mailbox, and, from the green plastic bin that hung just below it, plucked out the daily paper.

As she returned, she separated the sports and business sections from the rest of the pages. Halfway up the wide stone stairs to the porch, she handed them to Jeff, who, with David, had come out of the house. "Who was that?" he asked her, and they grinned at each other at his nosiness. So few pedestrians passed their house that those truly rare occurrences became something of an event, and were a bit of a joke between them.

"Mrs. Emenesky." Jeff looked blank, so she prodded, "The lady in the house down the road. She asked how I liked it here, and I told her I loved it. That it was wonderful, always feeling so safe."

"Safe from everything but me," Jeff agreed, giving her an exaggerated leer.

Frances laughed, kissed her two darlings, and, as they returned to the house, got into the secondhand Chevy station wagon they'd bought for her after they'd moved out here. More than a year ago now, she told herself. *Thirteen months. Thirteen months of paradise.* As she pushed the key into the ignition, she took in the tidy, 150-year-old farmhouse, with its sparkling white clapboard siding and jet-black shutters, then looked forward, allowing her eyes to once again lovingly trace the small wooden bridge at the end of the driveway, the rushing brook beneath it, the putting green-like lawn on its border, and the sloping wooded hill just beyond. There was another hill behind her, just as thickly wooded. *Total seclusion,* the real estate ad had read, and it had been true.

There were no houses in sight of theirs, the only one possibly visible hidden by the thick, richly green foliage. Even in winter the denuded trees revealed only a hint of it, three hundred feet up the road. Mrs. Emenesky's home, the nearest to them in the other direction, was a hundred feet from the road, high atop the hill, perennially screened by huge evergreens.

Paradise. Certainly more paradise than anyone had the right to expect these days. Occasional cars and trucks rumbled by their home, and once or twice a day a jetliner flew low enough to be heard. Those few sounds were all that broke the blissful silence. The local paper recorded an occasional murder or robbery, but in each case it was a consequence of human nature; not a result of desperate, vengeful poverty, or the insanity and raging needs triggered by drugs.

Frances, feeling happy and grateful, her feelings intensified by the encounter with Mrs. Emenesky, backed out of the graveled drive and headed toward the nearest stores, which were contained in a small mall, four miles away. She drove down the road, past the crossroad, through the tiny town half a mile past it —a scattering of barely twenty houses—and turned onto the main highway, another two-lane affair. Glancing to her right, she could see the river that ran alongside. It sparkled in the sunlight and was so clear, she knew, that even in the deepest spots you could see straight down to the bottom.

She found herself enjoying the ride to the mall, as she always did, except when the hilly, sharply curving roads were snow-covered, or icy. The air was warm, soft with a gentle humidity; pleasant on the skin. Puffs of white floated in the serene blue sky. Like the fields that surrounded them, scattered houses stood gleaming in the sunlight, refreshed by the previous night's rain.

In the odd, sudden way things sometimes happened out here—lonely country roads unexpectedly opening up onto a huge sweep of hundreds and hundreds of new houses—a field of young corn abruptly fell away, its border sharp-edged by the asphalt expanse of the mall. Frances slowed, then turned to the left, into the huge lot.

The mall itself was small, as malls went these days. There was Jamesway, the K mart of the area—a quasi-department store containing mainly low-priced, low quality items—the Hudson City Savings Bank, a Radio Shack electronics shop, Cattelano's Pizza restaurant, CVS—a chain drugstore—a dry cleaners, a card shop, a small furniture store, a liquor shop, and one of the flagship supermarkets in the Shop-Rite chain.

Shop-Rite was her goal. She loved the huge supermarket—a building the size of a football field, and filled to the brim with an astonishingly wide array of foods; many of them exotic items she'd never hoped to see again once she and Jeff moved here from Brooklyn Heights.

As she unfastened her seat belt, she glanced down at her blouse. *Oh Jesus*. A stain. *Purple*. She'd had blueberries on her cereal. Must have spilled some as she ate. Automatically, she looked in the rearview mirror. *It figures*. Her hair was a bit of a mess, too. Nothing like country living. Already she was turning into Frances the Rube. But she smiled to herself as she fluffed her hair as best she could and then got out of the car; what difference did it make? She wouldn't run into anyone she knew. Nevertheless, she decided to keep her sunglasses on. Couldn't hurt.

Outside the store, she found one of the few free shopping carts. The rest, she knew, were already inside, creating the usual weekend tangle. She placed her newspaper in the cart's seat and pushed her way past the sliding glass doors, which opened automatically at her approach.

Inside, Frances threaded her way through the welter of carts and bodies, doing her best to hurry. Jeff had been agreeable when, before they'd married, long before David was born, she'd told him she didn't want to work after she had her first child. But when the time came, Frances had found that for all his modern thinking, Jeff was as traditional in his instincts as she in hers.

He liked having her home, he liked her doing all the domestic tasks. In those rare times when they fell to him, such as now, tending to David, she thought she detected a certain veiled resentment.

Not that, if she were right, she could quite blame Jeff. He worked hard during the week, and David, not yet two and already able to string together an amazing series of sentences, was at the age of nonstop investigation and experimentation; not the best sort of child for a father who longed to spend his weekends in a semi-supine position.

Flounder for tonight; London broil for tomorrow. Don't forget the milk, or you'll be back an hour from now. And salt. We're almost out of salt. She moved purposefully from one end of the store toward the other, this time managing to get it all done without having to backtrack.

Miraculously, when she reached the checkout area,

Frances found a line with only two shoppers ahead of her, one of them nearly done. She halted, pulled her newspaper out and opened it.

She laughed at herself as she did it, laughed at the smugness she was feeling. It was her own little discovery; having the paper to read made the frustration of waiting in line melt away. She was getting something done, not losing precious time. The smugness came because she'd never seen anyone else with the same idea.

Frances' eyes swept over the front page, taking in the headlines and the opening lines of their stories. An investigation was being promised on the downgrading of Fort Dix. A corporation was going to refund millions after being caught in a price-fixing scheme. An aquifer two counties away was being tested for possible contamination. She suppressed a small yawn. Her eye flicked past a fourth headline, then returned to it.

It was about a murder.

Usually that sort of thing was of no more interest to her than the other stories had been. But this had happened nearby; just two towns away.

She read the first six words of the story. "The body of an unidentified woman," and then the checker cried out "Next!" Belatedly, quickly, Frances began to unload her cart.

The cash register was the talking kind, announcing the price of each purchase. It had been around long enough so that neither Frances nor the checker paid attention to it. As the items rolled past the checker, Frances quickly stuffed them into brown paper bags. When the total rang up, Frances glanced at the numbers showing in the computer, made out a check and handed it over. A few moments later she was on her way out of the store. The big clock near the exit told her it was ten-thirty. *Not bad.*

Frances had barely cleared the exit and swung the cart to the right, when her eyes widened. She stopped dead.

Then, abruptly, she turned away, her back deliberately to the parking lot.

She stood like that for several moments, her churning blood roaring in her ears. Shoppers coming from the store found their progress impeded by a woman standing in their way; they jerked their carts around her, some of them grumbling. She was unaware of all of it.

Finally, slowly, as if she were fighting her way out of a mist, she realized she was facing one of the store's huge windows. The sun was bright against it. Her gaze quickened, and she stared intensely into the shimmering glass.

It reflected the scene behind her perfectly; the mammoth expanse of asphalt choked with cars, men, women and children; green hills in the background, the crisp blue sky above them. Frances continued to stare into it for several more moments, her heart pounding, her face flushed and uncomfortable.

Finally, she turned. Self-conscious, constrained, feeling as if she'd quite forgotten how to walk naturally, she shakily made her way back to the station wagon. To her relief, she'd found the reflection hadn't lied. There was no longer any sign of him.

Without any conscious thought, she put her bags in the back of the wagon and got behind the wheel. *Terrence.* Even after all this time, she had recognized him immediately. Sixteen years. It had been *sixteen years*.

She was halfway out of the parking lot before she

realized that seeing him had thrown her into a state of shock. "And you're still there, you jerk," she muttered to herself, trying to shake the image off: the sight of herself in that first instant, seeing him, stopping short, swinging away abruptly, idiotically. *As if I were* ashamed, *for God's sake*.

She shook her head. No, not shame. It came to her all at once, the answer flowing through her, unyielding, irrefutable. Not shame. Fear.

Fear.

It was a fear she didn't want to think about. A fear of things beginning to chip away, of small cracks, hitherto unnoticed, minuscule fissures that ran almost imperceptibly all along and through what had seemed a rock-solid edifice.

Frances tried to push it away. Angrily she told herself it was because of the stain. The goddamned blueberries. Her hair. Sixteen years. Sixteen years between what she had looked like then and what she looked like now.

But it wasn't that. Not really. Hardly at all. It was *Terrence*.

This time as she thought of him, she saw him as she knew him those many, many years ago. Her mood changed. She was seeing it all again; that sweet, brief interlude; that time that had never gone away. Even when she thought it had. *Terrence*.

They'd both been kids: sixteen. She was living then in the Flatbush section of Brooklyn; just her mother, her sister Peggy, and her; Dad long gone. Flatbush: lots of trees, lots of concrete, more sky than you'd expect. There'd only been two real dates; *evening* dates. The rest had been their classes together, the walks to her home after school . . . that afternoon in the park.

And the time—another afternoon—when he'd walked all the way through the hurricane to her apartment house. He'd arrived soaking wet, that sweet, innocent, open-faced, yet somehow very masculine smile of his completely unaffected. Mom had been there, and Peggy, and he'd sweetly played games with them that whole afternoon. Then, when it had been time to go, he had blithely walked back into that swirling rain as if it weren't there. She had watched him from her window, the wind and rain beating against her face, watched him until he'd disappeared into the distance.

The station wagon continued to roll along the highway, unimpeded, no cars in front of it, no cars coming, allowing her mind to continue to drift.

And then the day he didn't come to school.

She'd called after she got home, and no one had answered. She'd tried again that night, and the next day, and the day after that . . . and all the others after. No word from him, no word *about* him.

After the first week, she'd gone to his family's apartment house. Their name was still on the letter box. But when she'd rung the bell above it, no one answered. The second time she came, almost a month later, the nameplate had been changed.

Hell, you loved the tragedy of it. Great stuff when you're sixteen, she told herself. Then, glancing again at her reflection, *True. But only half true. Don't get too goddam mature and cynical about it. You know what he was like.*

She felt a tear form. Just one, she told herself after

a moment. And then she realized it was enough; she might not be able to handle any more than that.

The road that led to her home was near, and she tried to force her mind off the subject. *That's what you do when you're thirty-two, kiddo,* she told herself, giving it a spin of toughness. *You get on with things.*

Frances made the turn and drove slowly over the old stone bridge and past the scattering of houses that made up the tiny village a mile from their home. Then past the crossroad, and Mrs. Emenesky's. Two hundred feet later she swung the heavy wagon into her drive. Concentrating very hard, very consciously, on what she was doing, she pulled on the brake and began unloading.

What with the trees and all the water, it was cooler here than at the mall, and Frances found herself grateful for that, felt the need to be soothed. She climbed the five wide stones that made up the porch stairs, and thought of her sister, and how lucky she was to have Peggy so near; just six miles away. A pleasant warmth flowed through her. Kid sisters came in handier than she'd ever thought they would, back in the days when all the world lay ahead of her. Peggy was always good to talk to. *And she'd known Terrence.*

As she groped for the handle of the screen door, Frances paused. *Is that why I just thought of her? Because of him?* Entering, she gave the swinging door an extra hard nudge with her shoulder, as if to dislodge the thought.

"Thank God." It was Jeff, greeting her as she entered.

"Our offspring keep your circulation going?" Frances asked, and was surprised to find that her smile was forced.

Her dark-haired, heavy-muscled husband seem to tread more heavily than she'd remembered as he followed her into the kitchen. As he spoke, the pitch of his voice seemed oddly irritating. "From the second you left. Just now I found him trying to stuff the kitten into the cab of the train I got him."

Frances stopped in the midst of her determinedly swift unpacking. Her face fell and she felt a stab of guilt. "Maybe he's too young," she said. "It never occurred to me. He's so bright. And so good with animals. But I guess we can't really expect him . . . I mean, he *is* so young . . ." She stared at Jeff. "Where is he?"

He shrugged. "Got me. *You're* home." His grin was boyish.

He'd abdicated responsibility, Frances realized, the moment she'd walked in the door, or even as he'd heard the wagon pull up. Telling herself that cursing under her breath would be childish and accomplish nothing, she silently swept past Jeff and hurried through the living room, past the dining room, and into David's sun-filled playroom. He was sitting on the floor, moving around some blocks.

"Hi, Mom," he offered nonchalantly, and continued playing. "The car's in the *elevator*," he announced, the last word in his sentence one he'd picked up that week, and obviously relished. It had the most syllables of any of his words so far.

Frances bent down and kissed the top of his head, soft blond hair against her lips, inhaled its sweet aroma. Immediately his hand reached up, clutched hers, and together the two of them began walking back to the kitchen. "I love Demmy," he told her firmly.

"I know you do," she nodded as they entered the

kitchen. "But you have to be careful with Demmy. He's just a little kitten."

David nodded. "Like David. He's just a little boy."

Frances glanced over at Jeff, to see if he'd heard, and was sharing her amusement and pride. But he was hunkered at the kitchen table with a mug of coffee and a huge doughnut. He was reading the sections of the paper she'd brought home. The rest of the groceries were still on the counter.

He glanced up. "You see this?" he mumbled. "The killing over in Medham?"

Frances nodded without interest, and, as David munched on a cookie, resumed putting away the groceries. But Jeff continued.

His mouth was full of doughnut as he read. "Nude. Not a stitch on her. Found her in one of those fields around Medham. Must've been dumped there. Strangled, it says."

Frances glared at Jeff, but he didn't seem to know or perhaps care that David was in the room. "Only a gold chain around her neck. Nothing else." He noisily turned several pages, then stopped at a page with a large photo. He slapped at the picture with his hand. "Wow. You see what she looked like? What a waste."

There were food noises as he spoke, smacking sounds, as if the account he was reading was a part of his meal, was something he relished at least as much as his doughnut and coffee. "Really crazy. So near to us," he muttered, seeming to linger over the story, as if reluctant to leave it. His eyes remained focused on what, from where Frances was standing, appeared to be a yearbook photo of the victim.

Shuddering with revulsion, Frances violently gathered up David, slid back the glass door that led to the patio, walked quickly down the patio steps to the driveway, turned left, and crossed over the little wooden bridge. She walked a few feet farther, away from the house, then stopped, her back to her home, totally oblivious to the beauty that surrounded her.

Oblivious to all but the fact that before she'd left the house that morning, she'd felt no hostility toward Jeff. Damn it, why was life like this? One minute everything perfect. And the next—a small incident, something stupid and unimportant, and suddenly all the things you'd submerged, glossed over, shrugged off, came flooding back at you, angering you, disgusting you . . . frightening you.

Chapter
2

Wʜᴇɴ ꜱʜᴇ ᴄᴀʟʟᴇᴅ ᴛʜᴇ ɴᴇxᴛ ᴅᴀʏ, ᴘᴇɢɢʏ ꜱᴏᴜɴᴅᴇᴅ
needy. When she arrived, the look on her face con-
firmed it.

Peggy, at five-foot-six, was an inch shorter than
Frances, and the tight wave in her thick brown hair
was natural. The two sisters were always startled when
people told them they looked alike; they saw no simi-
larities at all. Frances' face was a bit longish, Peggy's
broad. Frances' nose went with her face, Peggy's was
small, almost pug. Frances was willowy, Peggy an in-
heritor of the squarish frame their mother had had;
compact-looking, with full, rounded breasts. Each
woman was attractive in her own way, and each, being
sisters, mildly envied the other's looks.

It had been Peggy who'd found the area. She'd
moved out here because her husband's work was here.
And after Martin had disappeared, she'd remained.
He'd been gone three years now, but Peggy hadn't
moved. She already had a job as a special ed teacher,
but would have hung on anyway, still hoping that one
day her husband would turn up. Jeff's subsequent

switch to a New Jersey surety bond firm had thrilled both sisters; it had enabled the move out here, so near to Peggy's home, reuniting them.

They'd been closer than most siblings when they were young, perhaps because of the circumstances of their childhood. Dad had been in and out of hospitals from the time Frances was four. She and her mother and Peggy had moved into their grandmother's small apartment, and Mom had gone to work.

When Frances was seven, her father died. Two years later Nanna was gone, and they'd been forced to move to an even smaller, cheaper apartment two blocks away; just far enough away to cause friendships to fade and eventually die. Five days a week, from eight to six, the two small girls were motherless. They went to school together, Frances, the older one, responsible for carrying the house key. Coming home for lunch, they'd eat the sandwiches their mother had made them the night before.

They unlocked the door when they came in, locked it when they left, unlocked it again when they came home for good at three. At four-thirty they began to do what they could to prepare dinner, so there'd be less for Mom to do when she got home.

It was why Frances had determined that when she had children, she would stay home, make sure they had a "normal" life. She sometimes wondered if, conversely, that was why Peggy hadn't had children. Because she'd been afraid something would happen to Martin.

And something *had* happened to Martin. And though three years had passed since his disappearance, Frances knew that was why Peggy had come today.

Frances met Peggy as she left her car, hugged her, and kept her arm around her as they climbed the stairs to the house. Jeff and David weren't around; they'd gone off to the lumberyard. Some minor repairs had to be made to the door of their small, ancient barn. "Rough one, huh?" Frances asked her sister as they reached the porch. Her voice was tender and caring.

Peggy's voice when she answered was small, as if she were fighting to keep it from breaking. "Big sister can always tell, can't she?"

"Big sister's a moron most of the time," Frances demurred, as they entered the house and went on into the kitchen. "But she's always willing to try and help."

The kitchen was both Frances' and Peggy's favorite room: large and sunny, the brook visible through the windows and large glass sliding door, light dancing over the white Formica surfaces near the sink, the brick flooring and beamed ceiling giving the whole room warmth and intimacy. But today it had no visible effect on Peggy, her expression still doleful as she said, "No, I'm the moron. I should accept it. You know. Be a mature, rational adult. Admit that Martin left me. For another woman. That's all. The usual crap. Happens all the time. Why should I be any different?"

It was a time for just listening, so Frances, still looking at her sister, waiting for her to continue, walked over to the cupboard. She'd never much liked Martin, had never thought for a minute that he was the faithful type. Not that she had any evidence to go on then, and still didn't. She pulled two cups down from the cupboard and filled them with coffee.

"Okay, I knew he was unreliable before I married him," Peggy went on. "And he sure didn't get any more dependable afterward. Those quick little jaunts to Atlantic City, blowing his whole salary in a couple of hours . . . Jesus, the time he pawned all the jewelry I had except for my wedding and engagement rings— and that was because I had them on my fingers. Remember? Anyone but a moron would know a classy guy like that would be bound to toss me over sooner or later for some bimbo. But I can't believe it. I keep going around and saying to myself, what happened to him? What *happened*?"

Frances gazed sympathetically at her sister. "If only you knew something concrete. That's probably all you need," she offered, hoping this time she'd somehow say the right thing, finally break the spell, get Peggy to drop the torch, accept the fact that no matter what had happened to Martin, the odds were enormous that it was nothing more than another woman, and that in any case he wasn't worth the heartache.

"Yeah. Concrete. You want to know something?" Peggy asked her, without waiting for a reply. "Sometimes I drive somewhere that's deserted. A wood maybe, or a lake, even a swamp. And I stop the car and get out and start looking around. Like somehow I'm going to find him lying there, where somebody left him."

The image of the girl in the paper flashed into Frances' mind . . . her battered body found in an open field . . . She pushed the thought away. "You're not doing yourself any good with that," she said softly.

Peggy gave a harsh laugh. "You're telling me. It's like a disease, only the kind that just gets worse when you pay attention to it. But sometimes I can't keep from doing it." Peggy shook her head and smiled wryly. "I mean, all this over a guy like Martin. *Martin!* It's not like he'd been Jeff. You know, a *real* husband."

Something about the words stabbed at Frances. She stared out the window. The view that had always warmed her was now just a view. Unseen cracks, microscopic fissures. There. Always there. *Growing.* She turned toward Peggy. She laid the words out like something on a table. Coldly, dispassionately. For all the world to see. For the first time. Because she had always pretended otherwise. "Jeff's not the paragon you think he is."

Someone else might have smiled, shrugged, or nodded in complicit amusement. But Peggy's eyebrows shot straight up. "You're kidding!" she said.

Frances felt herself squirming. But forced herself to say "No."

Peggy was genuinely stunned. "Jeff? Come on! If Sears-Roebuck had been selling husbands like Jeff, they'd never have had to reorganize!"

I'm just trying to make my little sister feel better. That's why I said it. Oh really? Well, she's been down like this before. How come you never said it any of those times? Frances thought of Jeff with David the day before, irresponsibly abandoning him the moment she'd come back. She again saw him savoring that newspaper story, gobbling it up like the junk he'd been stuffing down his throat. "He can be inconsiderate. He can be crude. And insensitive."

Peggy shook her head. "Have you gone off your rocker? Miss Bluebird of Happiness? To me you've always been the ideal goddamn couple. Five years you've been married. Five *years*. No fights I've seen or even heard about, never a single complaint. And it didn't look like you were living any kind of lie. I mean,

I'm no dummy about people. You know that. I swear to God, every time I visit you, I've felt like one of those poor kids. You know, the ones with the big black circles around their eyes, pinched little pale cheeks. I was just like them, pressing my nose against the window, looking in. Even *before* Martin dumped me. Or did whatever he did," she finished, gloom stealing back into her face.

Frances was feeling more and more uncomfortable, but she found herself pushing on, stubbornly. "I guess it's more since David was born," she said, her voice sounding all wrong to her as she spoke. "He's—I don't know, sometimes Jeff acts like a spoiled kid."

"Yeah, right. Well, he's an American male, isn't he? He's supposed to be like that." Peggy's look turned angry. "Jeez, Frances, I've never met a nicer guy in my life than Jeff. I'm sorry you're feeling this way, but anytime you want to dump the bum, I'll be glad to recycle him. Dig my fingers into that nice thick jet-black head of hair of his. Just kidding," she added quickly, obviously feeling she might have gone a little too far.

But Frances only half heard. An image of Terrence, seeing him the day before, had flashed into her mind. She looked at Peggy, about to tell her. *But Peggy might think that that and my complaints about Jeff are related. She's still got traces of her old psych major.* She pushed aside the cracks, the fissures. Tried to convince herself. *All I'm really trying to do is get her mind off herself, let her know that no one's life is perfect.*

And she seemed to have achieved that object. As Jeff's Toyota pulled into the driveway, Peggy laughed a little and said, "Hey, you know what? I just realized

I'm feeling a whole lot better now. Frances the Brainy. You big sisters sure know how to take care of runts like me. Thanks for lying a little about Jeff. That got the old juices going."

The two sisters spent the rest of the day together after Jeff and David came in talking and playing games with David, who adored Peggy. They had the radio on, and twice Frances heard what she thought were further reports on the killing in Medham. But the others were talking and she couldn't be sure. Not that it mattered. Jeff was in the room with them and nearer to the radio, but whether he didn't hear or had simply lost interest in the subject, he gave no indication of paying attention.

Several times that afternoon she thought of Terrence, but the thoughts didn't stay with her the way they had the day before. Talking about Jeff as she had, knocking him off his pedestal, making him more human, seemed to have helped her as much as it had Peggy. He was, after all, a good husband, a good man, someone she liked and enjoyed. If things could be better sometimes, in some ways . . . well, whose life couldn't be better?

Three times that night she was jolted out of her sleep. Each time it was because of a nightmare. But when she tried to remember the contents of each, all that came to her was blackness.

Chapter
3

"I CAN'T BELIEVE MYSELF," FRANCES MUTTERED UNDER HER breath the following Saturday, half amused, half amazed.

She'd found she was timing her morning so that she would arrive at Shop-Rite at exactly the same time she had the week before. When she discovered, just as she was leaving the house, that David had had an accident, she practically flung him out of his underpants and into another pair, before leaving him with Jeff.

Finally in the car, she resolutely treated the whole thing as a joke. *Shows how humdrum a housewife you've become. Trying to spice up your life with fantasy lovers.*

Fantasy, because by now she'd half convinced herself it hadn't been Terrence after all. She'd only seen him—whoever it had been—for an instant, then had immediately gone into that humiliating little pantomime of hiding herself. The more Frances thought about how she'd reacted, the more she felt like a jerk. *Jesus, if it really was Terrence, and he saw me go into my act, no wonder he beat it the hell out of there.* She hadn't said a word to Peggy or to anyone else. *Who else could I tell? Mrs. Emenesky?* She'd have felt too much like a dope.

But when she got out of the wagon at the mall, Frances found, annoyance now mixing with the amusement, that she couldn't keep her eyes still. They darted everywhere, absurdly, intently. Not satisfied to stare to her left, straight ahead, and to her right, several times she caught herself turning and peering in the direction from which she'd come. Because he might have arrived after her. The act was mortifying, made her terribly self-conscious. But she did it anyway, three, four, five times. Then, as she yanked out a cart in front of Shop-Rite, she did it again, immediately after swearing to herself that she wouldn't.

Inside the store, she went out of her way to look at the huge wall clock and try to gauge how much time she had if she were to get out by ten-thirty. What she saw left her disheartened; the crowd seemed even thicker than the week before. And she had more to buy. A couple of passing men glanced at her, eyes widening, then quickly, furtively, shifting away. It was a hot day; in the nineties. She'd told herself that was why she'd picked out the dress she now wore: a light rayon, sleeveless, the skirt short, the blouse open at the neck, a trace of décolletage showing.

It was the first time she'd worn it this year, and she'd stood for some moments in front of the mirror, anxious, checking herself out fore and aft, reassuring herself that nothing had gone awry since the summer before; that nothing had thickened or begun to jut out. The perfect dress for a day this hot, she'd told herself forcefully, yet feeling a twinge as she passed Jeff on her way out of the house. As if somehow he might wonder why she'd have chosen this particular dress on this particular day. *Jeff? Think about something like that? You* must *be mad.*

The vegetable and fruits section was a logjam, and the checkout counters she'd passed on her way in had lines that seemed to stretch into the next county. *Damn.* As she waited in a totally clogged aisle for someone—anyone—to move a cart, she glanced furiously over her list, once, twice, three times, trying to decide what could be eliminated. There was a stir behind her, and she suddenly blushed. Now it was *she* who was holding up traffic. The carts ahead of her had moved without her noticing. Apologizing, embarrassed, she darted ahead.

Come on, Frances, she raged at herself as she got out of the way. *You're here to shop, not act like some moony schoolgirl.* Having mentally eliminated nearly half the items on the list, she began moving as swiftly as she could. Twenty minutes later, when she reached the end of the checkout line, she found she was almost ten minutes ahead of when she'd left the store the previous week. But there were seven people ahead of her, each with their baskets piled so high it looked as if they intended to make it through the Donner Pass with food to spare.

She took out the paper, tried to concentrate on it, but it didn't work. Every few seconds she'd glance up and stare out the huge window in front of her, her eyes sweeping the giant lot outside. Startled, she realized—not certain when it had begun—that her heart was pumping as if she'd just run a mile. *I can't believe I'm doing this,* she told herself, and continued to do it, half amused by herself. Thirtyish, a wife, a mother, a deliberately innocent look on her face, peering here, there, everywhere—as if her glances through all the windows in the store were simply a part of her general, lively interest in her surroundings. *A woman of intense curiosity and great capacity to observe.* And then, five minutes later, less humorously, *I must have found the newest checker in the place,* she fumed to herself, amusement turning to impatient annoyance as she realized she was standing in the same spot she'd been on since she joined the checkout line.

Finally the people ahead of her began to inch forward, one customer, then a second, and then a third moving past the register. But there were still four ahead of her, and only three minutes to go. *Three minutes to go. To* what? *Come on, Frances,* she told herself for the hundredth time, *what makes you think for a second that he's going to be here at exactly the same time? Are* you *ever? Is* anybody? *Especially on a weekend?* But it didn't help. Her eyes now spent all their time alternating between the window and the Shop-Rite clock.

Ten-thirty came and went. With two people still ahead of her, the register had broken down, and it was taking forever for the checker to catch the eye of one of her superiors. Frances found herself wanting to scream. People on all the other lines around her had sailed right through. *Look, it probably wasn't him in the first place. In the second place, what does it really matter if it was?*

That seemed to settle her down a little, though she realized, to her chagrin, the fact that the register was working again may have helped calm her. But settled down or not, she still found herself staring through the window, close enough now to it that she didn't feel odd.

When it was her turn, a young teenage boy did her bagging. Frances found herself both grateful that she didn't have to distract herself by doing that chore, and wishing she had it to distract her. And then, finally, at last, *Eureka, caramba, and Happy New Year!* she was done.

Heat rose in waves off the asphalt and the variegated assortment of cars, trucks, and vans as she came out of the store. Looking around her, she glumly decided that never before had the people here looked so nondescript, so totally uninteresting. Keenly feeling a deep sense of deflation, she slowly, almost reluctantly, pushed her groceries up to the car. There had been no sign of him.

Grimly, grumpily, Frances stowed the bags in the wagon, and then straightened up, resolve shaping her mouth into a firm, straight line. She clanged the back door shut and began striding decisively toward the Jamesway. It was summer, and she had perishable goods in the Chevy, so she'd have to move quickly. But she *did* need a couple of things for the house, really *did*. It wasn't as if she were deliberately stalling, she told herself. Walking quickly, purposefully, she didn't notice that the half-humorous attitude she'd had toward all this was gone.

Once in Jamesway, she moved just as swiftly to the back of the store. The hardware section was there, and immediately she found the molly screws and heavy-duty staples she was looking for. In seconds she was at the checkout counter, and just minutes after that back at the car. All the way, she'd resolutely kept her eyes straight ahead. Still, the extra excursion filled her with guilt. Jeff worked so hard during the week; she really shouldn't have left him in charge of David for so long.

And of course, during these last few minutes, no matter how unswervingly she'd stared straight ahead, she'd still been looking.

Frances drove home, deliberately keeping the speed ten miles over the limit. It was home, she told herself, that counted now. Whether she'd really seen Terrence the week before or simply seen someone who resembled him, didn't matter. She was sure she'd never see him again, whoever he'd been. It was all over; a ridiculous flight of fancy that was now behind her.

Once home, she put away the groceries, then began making lunch. She was going to serve them all bacon sandwiches—Jeff's favorite—and then remembered, the thought jolting her. She'd passed up the bacon in her near-hysterical rush to get to the parking lot at the "right" time. Later, as Jeff ate his peanut butter and banana sandwich, she kept reading glumness, even suspicion, into his expression.

This is not an expiation—maybe, she told herself after finishing the dishes, a little of her humor returning as she began a general housekeeping she hadn't planned to do this weekend. She used the molly screws and the heavy-duty stapler, putting up a shelf and a backboard in the outer pantry, finally got around to cleaning out the fireplace, then firmly if reluctantly brought the vacuum down to the basement and got to work on all the accumulated dust, and the cobwebs that choked the rafters.

David played near her through all of this—he loved the cellar, especially since, when he played on it with his cars, its cement floor was so much like a road.

She gave him another treat. He also loved to explore. The cellar was a partial one; the area under David's playroom was a separate dirt-floored crawl space. For a while she'd wanted to check and make sure there was insulation under the flooring. Without it, when winter came, David, playing on the floor as he always did, could be susceptible to colds. It was a chore she could handle and thus spare Jeff.

They went outside. There were two window-sized openings at both ends of the playroom. Each was screened, with one of the screens removable. The openings were below ground level, with concrete-sided wells opening before them. "Would you like to go down there?" Frances asked, knowing the answer, getting it instantly in David's eager nod and simultaneous grin.

She'd taken a flashlight with her. She handed it to him, then lowered herself through the opening. "Please give Mommy the flashlight and then I'll help you in." Very seriously he handed it to her, then allowed himself to be lowered in. The beams above their heads were four feet from the bare dirt floor. Crouching, she shone the flashlight above her, while David kept remarking happily about the ground at his feet. "A house with dirt!" he informed her, surprised and impressed by the new experience.

There were battings of insulation throughout. It all appeared whole and secure. A good feeling, being able to check that off. She let David explore happily for a few moments more and then they climbed out and went back inside the house.

Miraculously, when it was time for his nap, he fell asleep almost immediately. Frances went into her bedroom, intending to lie down, but her eye fell on Jeff's chest of drawers. She'd been meaning to go through his things for some time; he held on to everything, no matter how ratty. Somehow it seemed as if everything would be put right—all the craziness of the past week laid to rest—if she did this now; took care of something more for Jeff, got his things in order while he was outside, doing lawn work.

She knew it wouldn't take long; one of his drawers was for socks, another for underwear; those two she always kept tabs on, and a third was the usual catchall where he kept his keys, his money, jackknives, flashlights, and whatever else seemed—at the moment he threw it in—to fit there. Jeff used another drawer just for his personal papers; his old college stuff, a few high school things, snapshots of his parents and siblings. She turned to the five remaining drawers, with their eccentric assortment of clothing.

The cliché, she knew, was that men can't bring themselves to throw anything away. Clichés had a dismal way of turning out to be true. In Jeff's case, she smiled to herself, it certainly applied. Frances began spreading out on the bed the things she hoped to discard, and in a few minutes she had a depressingly impressive pile. Depressing because she had a feeling most of it would make its way back into his drawers. She began to lie down, then changed her mind. She'd straighten out his catchall drawer, and the one with the papers. It would be a few minutes' work, and he might appreciate it. More important, it seemed, somehow, that doing it would tie up all the loose ends of the past week.

A few moments later she found herself wishing she'd never begun.

She'd found it at the bottom of his papers. A porno mag. Not just a *Playboy* thing; far worse then that. Wholly graphic, wholly ugly. She could only stand to take a quick flip through it; what she saw sickened her. Angrily, she replaced it; then, as a thought struck her, she retrieved it.

She turned to the contents page. But the sick feeling only intensified as she checked the date. This wasn't something left over from his high school days. This swill was only two months old.

Frances replaced the magazine, shut the drawer, and didn't bother straightening the other one. There was a small chintz-covered chair by the sewing machine in the corner, and she sat on it, huddled in it. *There's nothing wrong with it. The usual male impulse,* she tried to tell herself, convince herself. *They* are *different from us.* Maybe it was even something somebody had passed on to him, and he'd looked at it out of curiosity, then forgotten it. *Right. Fat chance.* She gazed down at the floor, trying somehow to make it seem all right. Oddly, she found herself thinking of Terrence.

Probably just the same, dammit. Maybe far worse. After all, how well had she really known him? Frances rose from the chair, determined to be over with it, to get on to something else. Still, she found herself hoping that Jeff didn't return to the house anytime soon. She didn't think she could stand looking at him, not for a while yet.

Chapter
4

SOMEHOW FRANCES GOT THROUGH THE NEXT FEW DAYS. BOTH nights of the weekend they were invited to dinner parties by couples they'd known in the city, and by the time they got home, Jeff was too tired to suggest love-making. The next two nights he was away on business.

She felt grateful the first night he was away. Welcomed his absence, hoped his being away would spark more positive feelings in her when he returned. Even his traveling, she hoped, would by itself make her feel more caring toward him. He hated to fly. It was the only thing she knew that, if not frightened by it, at least made him uneasy.

Jeff was a surety bond underwriter. She felt some small guilt that she'd never been able to quite understand exactly what he did, but she knew it had something to do with guaranteeing that huge construction jobs would be carried out satisfactorily. Jeff's company would stand behind whichever company won the bid, guaranteeing against any default. When jobs were too big—millions upon millions of dollars involved—then Jeff and his firm would seek what he called reinsurance—a split of the risks, and spoils—with other insurance companies.

It all sounded rather easy from what she understood of it, and Jeff more than once told her it was, but there were also tremendous pressures; one wrong guess on an outfit he'd bonded, and Jeff's company could lose huge amounts of money. Adding to the pressures were the straight insurance people affiliated with the parent company of his firm. Afraid of losing business from longtime clients suddenly turned down on a surety bond, they kept urging Jeff to bond the companies they sold insurance to, not understanding—or more likely, not caring—that if he made a mistake, it could cost him his job.

So between the pressures and his dislike of flying, the doleful, apprehensive look on his face as he left had already done much to ease her feelings toward him. The first night he was gone, Frances found herself sleeping soundly for the first time in more than a week.

The second night was something else.

The day itself hadn't gone well. David had been out of sorts all afternoon—something that was extremely rare for him—and had been an absolute horror at dinner, whining and pushing away most of his food. Afterward, it had taken her nearly a half hour to get him to sleep. Even then he seemed fitful.

Finally sure he was asleep, she retired to her bedroom, and, figuring it would be relaxing, decided to watch a documentary on the local PBS channel that sounded both interesting and undemanding. Switching the TV on a few minutes early, she found herself watching the last of the station's local news. She told herself later that was what probably started it all.

New Jersey rarely brimmed over with news. So it was no surprise when, despite the case being more than a week old, with almost nothing new to update it, they got on to the murder of the poor woman in Medham.

Unfortunately, showing the same photo that had run in the newspaper—it *was* from a yearbook—reminded her of Jeff's reaction. The victim had been twenty-two, born and raised in Medham. No one seemed to have a clue as to who could have killed her. The only new note, and a minor one, was that no one close to her could remember her owning the slender gold chain she'd had about her neck when she was found.

The news went on to other things, and then her show began. But after a few minutes she turned the set off. She'd become too agitated to watch, kept seeing the girl's face, and remembering Jeff's attitude toward the whole thing.

He'd said he wouldn't call tonight. Maybe she could just go to sleep early, clear her mind of all this. *Try some warm milk first. That should settle you down, help you to sleep.* She rose and went to the kitchen, poured some milk into a pot and turned on the burner.

The distraction of the activity itself seemed to help, and she was almost back to herself when she switched off the kitchen light and began to grope her way into the unlit living room with her milk.

Halfway into the room she stopped dead. There'd been a noise; a heavy, thumping sound. It seemed to have come from the front porch, just outside the living room.

Oh, Jesus. No noises. Not tonight, Frances told herself, trying to shake off the effect the sound had had on her. *I'm a city girl. Sometimes this damn country —all alone out here, no one to yell to, no place near to run to . . .*

She began to move forward, and then froze again. There was a creaking sound, as if whatever was on the front porch had shifted position. *Come on, it's nothing. A shutter banging, something like that.* She listened for wind, but there didn't seem to be any. *Well, maybe an animal. Or the damn house just adjusting itself.*

But the thought didn't help. Despite railing at herself for her stupidity, for her timidity, she found herself rooted. Then, just as she had dismissed the whole thing as nonsense, was about to walk to the couch and turn on the light, it came again. But this time it seemed to come from *inside* the house. As if whatever had been on the porch had silently stolen around her home and into—*where the hell is it coming from? The cellar?* She found the possibility at once ludicrous and hard to dismiss. There had been enough time between the last sound and this for it to have happened.

Furious with herself, Frances raised the cup to her lips, defiantly prepared to drink it down, bring the cup back to the kitchen, and then go on upstairs to bed.

That was when she found out how bad it was. When she tried to raise her arm, and couldn't. Because she was paralyzed by fear. Because the sound had come again, clearer this time. Though still tantalizingly hard to place, it seemed to her as if it might be coming from directly under her feet. She glanced toward the front door and remembered. Yes, she had locked it. Had *definitely* locked it. Remembered *doing* it. But the cellar door . . . the sliding door from the kitchen to the patio . . .

Swinging about abruptly, not giving herself time to think, she rushed into the kitchen, lunged toward the cellar door, tested it. Finding it was unlocked, she quickly turned the key, pulled it out and placed it on the counter. In two steps she reached the sliding glass door, pushed back on its handle. But it was already locked. For a moment she stood there, her heart pounding, cursing herself for being so foolish. And then for the first time she remembered him. *David.*

He was *upstairs. Alone.*

Shame filled her. She'd always believed, always been sure, that no matter what, her child was everything to her, that she would sacrifice anything, everything, for him. But in her anxiety and instinct for self-preservation, she had totally forgotten him.

Sick with herself, she wheeled, planning to go to him, rush up to him. And then once again found herself immobile. There'd been another noise, a loud cracking sound, perhaps from the back of the house.

She couldn't kid herself out of it, couldn't tough it out. The memory of the murdered woman, the total isolation and darkness that surrounded her, had paralyzed her with fear. Abject fear. Fear so overwhelming, she wondered if she could survive it. There was a rustling sound. This time, the blood pulsing through her, ringing in her ears, she couldn't place it even tentatively. But somehow it seemed *nearer.*

Frances glanced toward the living room. All she could see was a wall of black, the total darkness she'd have to go through to get to the equally darkened staircase. Because she was unwilling to turn on a light, unwilling to expose herself that way. In case whatever it was was *out there* now, *waiting, watching*.

Slowly, as quietly as she could, Frances started to move forward, and almost immediately stopped. A sound again. Faint. Soft. *Different*. And then she looked down and saw it was the milk in the cup, splashing faintly as her hand, clutching it, quivered. Slowly, fearfully, she tried to silently set the cup down on the nearby counter, gripped it with two hands in the hope that would stop the shaking, allow her to set it down without a clatter. A sob escaped her, shattering the silence, pinpointing her location. The blood draining from her, she set the cup down and clasped her hand over her mouth, as if somehow, by remaining totally silent, she'd be all right. She and *David*. *Dammit, don't forget your son*. Slowly, feeling her way, she moved out of the kitchen and into the living room.

The pitch of the floor was uneven in here and in the dining room. In the past, trying to grope their way to the stairs in the dark, she and Jeff had laughed helplessly as they found themselves way off target. Tonight the humor was replaced by fear that she'd bump into something, knock something over, reveal her whereabouts by doing it. She couldn't reach out for the wall as a guide; there were too many things in the way; fragile things, things easily sent flying.

Somehow she got through the living room, and then, her hand out before her, she found herself beginning to blunder into the dining room table. But she stopped in time, and felt a small feeling of relief come over her. She'd be able to use the table as a guide to the stairs; they were in a straight line with each other.

Seconds later she was at the foot of the stairs. Above

her the blackness yawned. Slowly, painfully, she began making her ascent, freezing each time a stair creaked. There had been no other sounds for some time now. Listening for them, straining to hear them, she found she could hardly breathe. Twice she teetered on the stairs and had to steady herself, press up against the wall.

Finally she reached the top step. Her body tensed, ready for an onrushing form hurtling toward her . . . But nothing came. Still standing there, she began to relax. And then the sound came again.

Where is it? Below her? Above her? Only inches away? This time she couldn't tell at all, shook her head in desperation.

Pushing herself forward, feeling her way along the wall—she finally found it: David's door. She lowered her hand to the knob and then began to turn it, slowly, so slowly, that the movement, if there had been light to see it by, would have been almost imperceptible. She felt the latch come free. Slowly, silently, she pushed the door open, pressed it into the waiting dark.

Her back against the door, Frances slid herself into the room, into the impenetrable darkness, then carefully closed it behind her. She felt for a key, but stopped herself. There *was* no inside lock. She'd had Jeff remove it when they'd come here, afraid David might somehow lock himself in.

She turned toward David's bed . . . and froze.

There was a form just beyond the bed, a hulking shadow half hidden in yet deeper shadow. Her breath caught, and a whimper of fear escaped her. And then her breath came back, as she remembered. The tent. Jeff had made David a tent out of a blanket stretched over two chairs. That was all it was. Her breathing suddenly became easier. She found herself able to turn on the light.

David lay fast asleep in his bed, serene, untouched, *safe*. And yet . . . the fear was still there. *Dammit, stop being such a sissy*. She turned off the light, whirled, walked out and closed the door behind her. She switched on the hall light, then all the other upstairs lights, checking in the guest room, the bathroom, her own room. Everything normal.

Everything bright and cosy and normal. It was all over. The feeling was gone. She'd been a fool, a total moron. She'd been that way, one way or another, for more than a week. But that was all over now. She neared the stairs. And then she stopped. This time, there was no mistaking it.

Someone was downstairs. There was absolutely no question. Those were footsteps. Heavy. Measured. Fear lodged in her throat, clawed at it. Hesitantly, awkwardly, her knees quivering, she backed toward David's room, squeezed the knob to the right, backed inside, closed the door as quickly and as quietly as she could. She raced to the bed, put her hand over David's mouth and pulled him out of bed.

The rustling noises of the covers and the movement of her own clothing cloaked the sounds downstairs—if they were still *downstairs*—The rustling rose over her so thoroughly that she heard nothing else. Heart straining against her breast, she moved in a half crouch to the furthest corner of the pitch-black room, found the chair she was seeking, slid behind it and then lowered herself and her child—her only child—to the floor. David cradled in her lap, she cowered there.

For the first time the idea of using the phone occurred to her. But it was in her bedroom. She'd have to go into the hall . . . might be heard. Almost certainly *would* be heard if she reached the phone, dialed it, began to speak.

Jeff. It might be Jeff. Maybe his trip had been cut short. He was due back tomorrow; maybe something had happened. *No.* She hadn't heard the Toyota come into the driveway. She'd have heard that, tires on gravel, the old familiar sound of his car. Familiar, *comforting* sound. She'd have heard it. She *would* have.

She gasped, her hand flying desperately to her mouth to cut off the sound. *The footsteps.* She heard them again. They were coming up the stairs. Slowly, heavily.

They reached the top of the landing, hesitated, then moved toward her bedroom. She heard its door swing open. She could leap to her feet, run into the hall and then down the stairs. If she were fast enough, she might . . . But if she weren't . . . Her grip on David tightened and she tried to shrink into herself, make herself smaller.

The steps were coming closer now. They stopped just outside the door.

Slowly, it opened. The light was still on in the hall. She could see a shape appear, black, featureless. Its hand went to the wall switch.

As the light came on, it took her a second to realize. For a moment it was as if she had never seen him before. And then it was plain, so plain . . . *Jeff.* "Jeff!"

He turned toward her, startled.

"What're you doing *there*?" he cried out.

Frances jerked her hand to her lips, indicated the

still sleeping David. Quickly, shakily, she rose, placed him in his bed, tucked him in. Then she turned toward her husband, ready to collapse into his arms. And stopped.

For the first time, she saw he had something in his hand.

It was the kitten. Its body was lifeless.

Bewildered, oddly frightened in a way she hadn't been before, she stared at Jeff. But she read nothing in his eyes. She signed to him, and together they silently stepped out of the room. Then, frantically, after she'd closed the door behind him, she whispered, "How did that happen?"

He shook his head impatiently, almost as if it didn't matter. "I don't know. The damn Toyota broke down a mile from here. Had to walk all the way. I found this by the front door."

He started to go on, but she interrupted him. "Inside it?" she asked, afraid of what his answer might be. "Inside the front door?"

"No. *Outside.*"

She snapped then, and, sobbing, flung herself against Jeff. Demmy had been in the house all evening. She was sure of that. There was no way he could have got out of the house. Unless someone *else*— someone who'd *also* been in the house, had killed it and then left it outside the door.

She shook and sobbed, her breath coming in great gasps. Finally it began to subside. She looked up at Jeff. He was staring at her strangely, the dead kitten still in his hand. *Well, of course he'd look at you that way. Coming home, finding you like this.* And then something stabbed at her, and she looked into his eyes

again, afraid of what she might see there. As if somehow he might have divined that as she'd clutched
him, a part of her had been holding onto him as if he
had been Terrence.

Chapter
5

In the next few days what had seemed bizarre and frightening had become something to laugh about, to shrug off. There had been nothing much wrong with the car; a loose connection, though the mechanic seemed puzzled that that particular wire should have worked itself loose. There was always the chance that someone at Newark Airport, where Jeff had left it, had fooled with the car, but that seemed unlikely.

David had cried when she told him about Demmy, but seemed all right shortly after, as if he understood and accepted it. And with Jeff home again, her fears hadn't returned. She managed to convince herself that she had been wrong. Demmy must have got outside himself, somehow, perhaps scurrying past her when she'd put out the garbage. After all, he had been very small, very easy to overlook.

And the noises she'd heard before Jeff came home —house noises, that's all that they were, she could now tell herself with almost total certainty. After all, they'd been ambiguous, hard to locate. As for the feeling she'd had, the feeling of being watched—*house-*

wife hysteria, she found herself able to shrug. So after two or three days, life resumed its normal shape.

The fourth morning, Peggy called from work. "Guess who I saw last night?" she asked, without any preliminaries. There was excitement in her voice.

"You got me. Who?" Frances replied, mildly curious.

"Terrence Horgan! The boy you went out with when we were living on East Twenty-third Street!"

Frances, starting to reply, found she was having trouble responding. The words seemed to be catching in her throat. "Where?" she finally choked out.

"Going to the movies at the Musconetcong mall. I had to pick up a prescription at the drugstore. And just as I passed by the movie house . . . there he was."

Frances' chest still felt constricted. "You're sure it was him?"

"Absolutely."

"Did you speak to him?"

"Dammit, no. But I definitely know it was him. No way I was wrong. Sometimes it seems like everybody in the world is moving to New Jersey." She paused, and then went on in another tone, her voice softening, becoming almost dreamy. "God, Frances, did I have a crush on Terrence. I remember that first date you had with him. I got to open the door, I guess because you didn't want to seem overanxious. He was so tall, and so good-looking. He smiled at me so sweetly. And that time he came over during the hurricane. Remember that?"

Frances gave her a quiet "Yes."

"You remember? We all played games? I played them, too. And he treated me just like I was an equal. There I was, a geeky little eleven-year-old kid, but the way he treated me, I could've been someone from high school. He didn't talk down to me, and I guess he realized we had the same kind of sense of humor—you know, when he kidded me, I could tell he knew I'd understand it was a joke and wouldn't get all huffy or stupid or anything."

As Frances spoke, she heard her voice go stiff. She'd felt oddly injured when Peggy talked about sharing the same sense of humor with Terrence. "You never told me. I had no idea you remembered him at all, let alone like that."

"I sure do. He was so sweet. And bright. And so cheerful." She sighed. "Even now, when I think about him, he seems like the nicest boy I ever knew. Ever *could* have known."

"He was," Frances answered quietly.

Peggy didn't stay on the phone long after that, and Frances was grateful, finding she couldn't concentrate on any of the rest that followed. As soon as she hung up, she dressed David and hurried out to the car with him. Then she drove toward the Musconetcong mall.

Chapter
6

WHERE'S THE GUILT? FRANCES TRIED TO KID HERSELF AS she headed toward the mall. To her surprise, she felt none, felt no furtiveness, no sense of betrayal. *Because of David, maybe.* Hard not to feel safe, housewifely and mundane, with a kid in the backseat. *No femme fatale behind the wheel.*

But she did feel oddly young. Like a teenager, gigglingly driving past the house of the high school football captain. Not that she'd ever done a thing like that in her life. No car in Brooklyn, and she couldn't picture herself having done it anyway. But she'd heard of other kids doing it; driving all over creation on the billion-to-one chance they might spot their fantasy dreamboat.

She sniffed in annoyance as the last words crossed her mind. No. Terrence wasn't like that; he wasn't somebody made up out of whole cloth. She'd *known* him. All the things she thought about him were true. Hadn't her own sister just echoed her feelings?

But still. The rest of the teenage analogy did hold true. Drive thirty-five miles in the crazy, impossible hope that she'd see him—and then do nothing more than that. Not even stop. *Well, maybe I'd stop,* she corrected herself, *but that's all. I'd stop far enough from him so he couldn't see me. Watch him from a safe distance. Still in the car, my hand over my face, just in case he glanced my way.* She sighed. *So that's why I don't feel any guilt. Because that's all this is, just a kid's kind of thing, something to amuse myself with. Doesn't mean anything.* She punched on the radio, twisted the dial till she found a rock oldies station. *There. Just to make it completely adolescent.*

Nearly an hour after leaving her house, she reached the mall. It was a new one—she'd only been there twice before—mammoth in size. There were three name department stores, each two stories of sprawling concrete and glass. The separate, enclosed mall contained even more glass, even more concrete, even more space. In addition there were stores that fronted on the main building, and, scattered around the vast acres of asphalt, individual restaurants and movie buildings. It took her nearly fifteen minutes to circle the whole area. Then, laughing a little to herself, she began to do it again.

There was a small noise beside her, and, startled, she turned toward David. As she glanced at him it occurred to her that he'd been unusually still through all this. Ordinarily he chatted away, enthusiastically reporting on everything he saw. But now as she gazed at him, she saw he was still quiet. His eyes were fixed on her.

As if he knows.

Squeezing the wheel, she shook her head. *Don't do that. Don't think that. Don't be such a jerk. He isn't even two, for God's sake.*

Slowing the car, she turned back toward David. She'd talk to him, be light and motherly, break whatever stupid spell this was. But she found she couldn't. Fretfully, she turned away and picked up speed. From the corner of her eye she could tell he was still staring at her.

This'll be the last time, she told herself, fighting a weakening of her will. *Go all the way around one more time. Then you'll be done with it. It'll be out of your system. The last time today, the last time ever.*

And then, when she had passed the last building and was back where she'd started from, she found herself doing it again. *Hey, just one more time . . . what difference can it make? Indulge your idiotic fantasies, or whatever they are. It can't hurt, can it? It can't hurt anything at all,* she told herself, resolutely keeping her eyes away from the silent child beside her.

Halfway through the third go-round, she saw him. There was no question this time.

Terrence. He had just got out of his car. He was heading toward a bakery that fronted on the mall.

He was still as tall and as straight as ever. His once-blond hair retained tinges of gold. Even from this distance—she was almost forty feet away—the gentleness that had been so much a part of him was still marked on his features. And his walk—that walk of his that had so amused her way back then, the walk of an adolescent proudly getting the most out of his newly long legs—that walk was still as brisk and purposeful.

Frances watched him until he disappeared into the bakery, the reflection of the shop's large glass window hiding him from her sight. *There. You've done it. Now let's get the hell out of here.*

Then she remembered. Her lips twisted wryly.

She'd promised Jeff she'd get him some cake for dessert. As the thought came to her, she barely heard the announcement on her radio. A second woman had been found strangled in a nearby town.

When Jeff came home that night, David ran up to him, as he did every evening. "Daddy, Daddy, a man from the bakery talked to Mommy!"

Instantly, Frances felt the burning in her face. She threw her hand up, half covered her face, trying to hide the flush she was almost certain was staining her cheeks.

But Jeff appeared to react as any husband would have. "Oh, really?" he answered his son, swinging him up into his arms, glancing at Frances with apparent amusement. "And just what was the man telling Mommy?" But David was already jabbering away about a dog he'd seen near the house that afternoon, describing it with great explosions of enthusiasm, and that appeared to be the end of the topic of the Man from the Bakery Who Talked to Mommy.

Jeff was a Mets fan, and there was a ballgame on TV that night. He went into the bedroom to watch, happy about the game, grateful that it would give him a chance to relax, forget about work. During dinner he'd reported that things were a bit touch-and-go in the office. A couple of companies he'd underwritten were looking shaky.

David was already in bed. Frances, having finished the *New York Times* that Jeff brought home from work every day, found herself a book and seated herself on the living room couch with it.

She opened the book, but didn't pretend to read, not even the first few words.

She wanted to recapture that afternoon, every detail of it, all over again, as she had on the drive home; in brief moments as she'd prepared dinner; while doing the dishes; as she got David ready for bed. This time she could do it without any distractions, give herself up to it completely.

After her air-conditioned wagon, the intense heat of the midday sun had been startling, nearly staggered her. With the still strangely silent David in her arms, she'd walked a few steps toward the bakery, and then stopped.

To go in, find herself stared at by the people there while she and Terrence exchanged greetings . . . the blitheness she'd felt till then suddenly fell away. She couldn't do it. Not that way.

Instead, she walked up to the huge mall building, stood in the shade of its overhang, a little to the side of the bakery. If he mentioned he'd seen her standing out there, she'd say she was waiting for a friend. Otherwise, as he exited, she'd walk toward him, then cry out, immediately express her astonishment at "bumping into" him.

The wait had seemed to go on forever, David not making it any easier. His continued silence unsettled her, and his eyes still didn't leave her. She'd placed her hand on his forehead, but it was cool. Nothing about him had suggested illness. Once she tried pressing his head to her breast, out of her line of sight, but he'd resisted.

Then he'd come out of the shop, a bag of bread under his arm.

"Terrence!"

He'd spun and looked puzzled for an instant. She remembered she was wearing sunglasses. She removed them and his eyes had opened wide. Something sprang into them, something hungry, yearning.

Despite her plans, she'd immediately found herself abandoning any pretense of this being an accident. The words spilled out of her so quickly, so breathlessly, that she wasn't sure that he ever did quite comprehend.

Again she tried to force herself to remember precisely what she'd told him, but once more they came out in a jumble. Whether more or less jumbled than in actuality, she didn't know. "I knew it was you. I saw you at the Shop-Rite and I, well, I didn't know—and then Peggy—you remember, my sister, she was just a little girl when you knew her—she said she'd seen you here . . . and I, well, I got in the car right after she called, and I kept driving around, and then I saw you going in the bakery, but I decided to wait, and I, well, I wasn't supposed to tell you any of this, but here I am doing it . . ."

Seated on the couch, the open book still in her hand, she found herself squirming, thinking of the fool she'd made of herself. *What a jerk, what a total jerk!* But . . . he hadn't seemed to notice, or if he'd noticed, hadn't cared. He'd barely taken his eyes off her all the time they spoke. Only once, really, and then to admire David, her child.

His voice—the voice that had sent shivers down her spine even before they'd dated—was as rich and as deep as ever. And, she found, still as thrilling to her. And his hair, his eyes, his nose, his lips, those lips of his . . . *And he looked at me exactly the way I must have been looking at him.*

Yet somehow the conversation had been awkward, forced. Maybe it was the people walking by, maybe it was having David in her arms, reminding her, reminding them both, of the time that had passed, the time that could never be made up . . .

God. She put down the book. *What else could you expect? He was a teenage romance, for Chrissake. That's all it was . . . raging hormones, and the novelty—yes, the* novelty, *damn it, of newfound feelings.*

But telling herself all this did no good. She found herself drifting away, feeling all over again what she'd felt as they'd stood there, the two of them.

Terrence had always been extremely capable, with an artistic flair, and that had carried over into his career. He was an industrial designer, he'd told her, for some giant corporation she'd never heard of—worldwide, he'd said. They'd transferred him out here—his office was ten miles away—three weeks before. He was living in a motel room for the present, till he found a place.

"Why don't you—" she'd begun. She'd been about to invite him to get together, to come for dinner, maybe even to stay with them till he got himself settled. But Jeff's face had flashed before her, and somehow it had seemed all wrong that way. Instead she'd broken in on herself, goofily shoved her watch up to her face and immediately announced in a high, choppy voice—*did it really sound as bad as I think it did?*—that she hadn't realized it was so late, that she had to get going, that it was wonderful having seen him. Then, before he'd had a chance to reply, she'd turned and rushed off into the bakery.

Inside it, she hadn't once looked out the window, had forced her eyes away. Had he stood there and watched till she disappeared through the door? Had he lingered, hoping she'd be out soon? She'd deliberately let a few people go before her, pretending to be unable to make a choice. And when she'd finally come out, he was gone.

Frances put the book down. With a jolt she realized it had never occurred to her to notice what Terrence's car looked like. She shook her head angrily. *So what? You're not looking to find him again. You saw him, you spoke to him, and that's it. Be grateful for that. Now get on with your life.*

She could tell that the Mets game was still on, the faint sound of it trailing its way down the stairs. Frances sighed, shrugged, and climbed the stairs.

She went into the bathroom first, got herself ready for bed. When she entered the bedroom, Jeff told her, half apologetically, "Just the top half of the ninth to go, probably. The Mets are ahead, 5–3." She nodded, and slid into bed. He always told her how his team was doing. Even though she knew nothing about baseball, had never been able to get interested in it the few times she'd tried. His telling her was a little joke between them, but she knew it was something else, too. It was something that was important to him. And because she, too, was important to him, he felt the need to communicate it to her.

There was a commercial on. Jeff glanced toward her. "Seems our little corner of the world is getting famous. They had a newsbreak. About that second girl you mentioned. They found her in Allenville. And it was like the other one. Dumped in a field. Strangled. No clothes on."

Frances nodded, already sleepy, her mind on something else. Terrence had told her he wasn't married. Not anymore. Had told her that while he was looking at her in exactly the same way she was looking at him.

There was something more. He had told her why his marriage hadn't worked out. Because he hadn't married his wife for what she was. He had married her because she had reminded him of her.

Chapter
7

IT WAS STILL LIGHT AS FRANCES AND JEFF DROVE OVER the small iron bridge that spanned the Delaware. Reaching the other side, Jeff steered south, onto the narrow, picturesque road that ran alongside the river, the road that would take them all the way to the inn they were headed for.

When Frances asked her sister if she'd mind keeping David for the weekend, it was almost as if Peggy had known. The look in her eyes seemed to say that she understood, understood perfectly.

Paranoia, it's my damned paranoia. That's all it can be. Uncertainly, Frances stared out the window at the scraggly woods to the right, then to the broad, clear river on their left.

We need to get away, she told herself. *Or at least I do. With Jeff. To put it all together again. To forget Terrence. Erase him.* To stop wondering if—when David had screamed out about the man in the bakery —Jeff had noticed her blush. *Had* she even blushed, or had she just felt that she had?

And she had to stop wondering if David had said

more when he and Jeff were alone. If Jeff had pumped him. *But then how much more could he have said? He's so little—so proud that he could say a word like "bakery" to his Daddy.* That's all that was; that's all he could possibly have remembered—or understood. And yet . . . he'd been so *silent* in the car during the time she'd searched for Terrence. Even on the drive back home . . .

She closed her eyes, forced them shut, tightly, then reopened them. *Looks like it's not just Jeff I have to fix things up with. I've got to stop feeling this way about poor David, too.* Feeling suspicion—even hostility—toward her poor little boy, her sweet little boy. She felt sickened by herself.

Jeff had turned on the car radio, pushed the volume up. A barely intelligible squawking crackled from the speakers, assailing her ears. "Can barely get the Mets here," he apologized. "I'll just keep it on till I hear a score—don't want to drive you crazy with it."

She smiled and dropped her hand down on his thigh, then kept it there. It was the way they usually drove. As she did it, she realized it had taken her till now to do it; nearly an hour since they'd left the house.

"I'm so glad you wanted to go away, too," she told him.

"Hey, I can use it. We *both* can use it," he answered, glancing quickly at her, then away.

What does he mean by that?

The doubt angered her, shook her. Even more angrily, she did her best to dislodge the thought. *Ask him about his work, for Chrissake. He needs to talk about it, and you need to listen. You've been too damn preoc-*

cupied with yourself. You can't keep a marriage going that way. "Anything much happen on your trip?"

He glanced at her. "You interested, or just making conversation?" He said it lightly, as if either was okay with him. But of course he didn't wholly mean it that way.

"I'm interested. It occurred to me you hadn't had much to say about it. Mainly, of course, because of all my craziness that night you got back."

He nodded, patting her hand. "Well, it's the same old Texas stuff, that's part of it." He nodded toward some people floating down the river in tire tubes, pointing them out to her. "That new atom smasher they got going down there. The college one. Nothing really happening. It's just public relations stuff. You know, I visit the site, I look at the construction company's equipment and act like I understand what I'm seeing. All I really need to do is stay in the office, study their financial statements and figure out their net quick. In fact, when I got back on Tuesday, I told Doughty—"

"Wednesday," she interrupted him.

"What?"

"You got back home Wednesday, not Tuesday. Unless you're leading some kind of a double life, or something."

He shrugged, and half smiled. "Oh. Right. Anyway, when I saw Doughty, I told him the whole thing had been a waste of time."

"What'd he say?" she asked, a little afraid.

"Agreed. Said it sure was. But also said I should know by now that sometimes the chickenshit stuff pays off more than all the sitting around on your butt pumping a calculator."

"Sounds as if he got a little cranky," she suggested tentatively.

His eyes flicked at her. "That's why I need to get away. Stop thinking about work."

She could see his worry, and was determined to do the best she could to bring him out of it. She'd sensed from the beginning that the chemistry between Jeff and Doughty wasn't right. She lowered her voice, made it soft and slinky, ran her hand along his thigh as she told him, "Okay. I'll do my best to get your mind off it."

The Bucks County inn where they'd reserved their room was the same one they'd been going to ever since their honeymoon. The oldest part of it, a two-story building, dated back to the 1700s and looked it: weathered, unpainted shingles, hand-blown glass in the windows, a nicely ancient chimney. They'd stayed in one of its rooms once, but they preferred the newer units because they offered more privacy. Single one-room buildings, their look was rather Rustic Motel, but the interiors were nicely countryish in an Old American way, and just primitive enough to seem restful and shut off; no phone, TV or radio. It was the first time they'd been back since David's birth, and as Frances looked at the hooked rug, the high-off-the-floor maple bed, and the old oak dressers, she found a store of memories flooding back, all of them good ones.

They made love almost as soon as they entered the room. And then again.

When he finally rose and began to get ready for dinner, he told her, "You've always done wonders for my appetite."

"*Appetites,*" she corrected dreamily. "You have, too."

They drove to what had been their favorite restaurant in the area; a cosy, low-roofed affair with substantial drinks and excellent, imaginative food, but to their dismay it was closed; out of business. But within minutes they'd found another; a newly opened spot in a wonderfully picturesque old stone building. It specialized in French cooking, and to their relief they found the food was wonderful; even better than the old place's, and they split a bottle of equally good wine over it.

When they returned to their room, they were feeling satisfied and mellow, and made slow, languorous love. "Ever notice how much easier it is when there's no little kid around?" Jeff kidded just before he fell asleep.

They made love again in the morning, and then had breakfast at the inn, something they looked forward to every time they came here. The dining room overlooked both the Delaware and the picturesque canal that ran alongside it. The food was nothing special; basic stuffs, buffet style, but it was always very fresh, and temptingly abundant. Crocks of hard-boiled eggs, tray after tray of just-baked Danishes—cherry, cheese, apple, blueberry. Steaming hot rolls and biscuits, thick jars of creamy butter, silver bowls brimful of home-made preserves, large stainless steel urns of excellent coffee, hot water for tea, huge jugs of milk . . . sturdy crockery and white linen tablecloths and napkins. "Wish I were a teenager again," Jeff said, polishing off his third Danish, "so I could really do all this justice."

"You're doing okay," Frances kidded him, her spirit

light. *It all seems to be working,* she told herself with relief.

After breakfast they strolled along the narrow, grassy strip of land between canal and river. They passed small homes that stood with their backs to the canal, most with boats of one sort or another in the backyard, or tethered in the canal itself. A spell of peace was on it all, the blissful silence broken only by the songs of birds and the rustle of the nearby river.

Occasionally they stopped and watched the Delaware. Even this far south it seemed totally unspoiled. When the light was right, they found they could stare six feet or more straight down to the bottom. *Like home,* Frances thought, comforted by the idea.

She looked up at Jeff. No question. This had been the right thing to do. It was like old times again, just the two of them, feeling and acting the way they always had when they'd been here. *So it had nothing to do with Terrence after all,* she told herself, sure now that everything was all right. *It's just been all the mundane things about married life. Sooner or later, someone has to take out the garbage. And that's hell on romance.*

That afternoon they went antiquing, and Frances found a small end table she knew would fit perfectly in an unused space just beside the front door. It was a steal at the price, and when she looked at Jeff, he grinned and said "Sure." As they left the shop, purchase in tow, he gave her arm a squeeze, and that seemed to be the last little thing she'd needed. *I'm all right now,* she told herself. *I'm all right from here on.* She felt so good she came very near to telling Jeff about Terrence, and all her consequent silliness. But on second thought it felt a little premature. *Maybe some other time.*

That evening they ate dinner at their inn. Saturday night was the night the owner oversaw the preparation of his own special steak recipe, a recipe that was a longtime favorite with Jeff and Frances.

They dined late, ate slowly, and splurged by finishing off dinner with dessert, coffee, and a liqueur. Frances fell asleep before Jeff even came to bed.

The dream, when it came, was nothing much at first. She was wandering along a lane. The grass was soft, and as Frances looked about her, she saw she was high atop a hill, so high that all she could see in the distance was sky; a sun-filled blue through which drifted small, white puffs of clouds. At her feet there were wildflowers, golden and delicate. But then she noticed the silence. No birds, no stir of wind. A path appeared, and she began to walk along it; even her footsteps made no sound. A feeling of unease began to grow in her.

The feeling was faint at first; a wisp of disturbance. Something was askew, not the way it should be. But she couldn't decide what it was, or even where it was: in the world around her or in that other world inside her. The uncertainty began to turn to frustration and fear. She felt a pressure slowly form around her skull, a band that pressed inward, tightly, more and more tightly. Without her noticing, night had fallen, and when she tried to peer ahead of her, she could see nothing but total, impenetrable blackness.

All she knew was that she was at a great height, pressing forward along an unknown trail that could, at any moment, end precipitously. But she found she couldn't stop, kept up her steady pace, despite the growing uneasiness, despite the ever-tightening pressure that threatened at any moment to crack through the frail margins of her outer and inner self. All at once, without warning, a wind came up, a shrieking black wind. It began to whip at her. The earth beneath her feet became moist, uncomfortable. Still she continued to move forward.

The grass disappeared, and her feet, now bare, found themselves treading over rock. It was cold and wet and slippery, and she sensed it would soon end. But she didn't hesitate, didn't slacken her pace, continued to point forward into the wind that howled about her, slashed at her face.

Suddenly she stopped. All at once she *knew*. Knew what was wrong.

Jeff was gone. He'd been with her. He should have been with her still. But somehow he was gone. She had no idea where he'd gone or why. *Jeff.* She opened her mouth to cry out for him.

But as she did the sky broke open. Light shattered through it, a light like nothing she'd seen on earth. In that moment she saw Jeff. He was standing only yards away from her. He was on the utmost brink of a cliff. His back was toward her. His arms were raised.

It took a moment for her eyes to clear, for her to see what he held above him. It was David.

Their child was screaming and kicking, crying out in terror for his mother. She yowled and sprang forward, arms outthrust in desperation, trying to save her child before Jeff drew his arms back and then flung them forward . . .

"Ahhhhh!"

Frances sprang bolt upright in the bed. For an instant she gazed wildly about her. Then she realized.

She'd screamed in her sleep, awakened herself. Shuddering, remembering the dream, she reached out for Jeff. Her hand met only the sheet.

She reached out again, farther, then swept her hand over the bedclothes. He wasn't in bed. Her eyes sought the bathroom, located it. There was no telltale light at the bottom of its door.

"Jeff?" she called softly, and reached for the overhead lamp. The light revealed an empty room. Uncertainly, she left the bed and went to the bathroom door, slowly pushed it open, afraid she might find him there, slumped on the floor, victim of a heart attack or stroke. But the room was empty.

Stumbling her way back toward the bed, she picked her watch off the bedstand and glanced at it. Almost five in the morning.

Frances strode to the window, pulled back the curtains and looked out. But even after she turned off the room light, she found it was too dark outside for her to see anything much. Even the form that she thought was their car was too buried in blackness for her to be sure.

Maybe he couldn't sleep. Took a walk.

But that wasn't like Jeff. She thought of calling the desk. But she didn't want to be ridiculous, or annoy anyone. The poor clerk was probably asleep, and there was, had to be, a simple, very prosaic explanation for Jeff's absence. It would all be very logical when he came back, the way things always turned out to be when you were faced with an unknown that made you worried and uncertain.

She went back to bed and sat there for nearly twenty minutes, her spine pressed tight against the headboard. Alternately she worried and chided herself for worrying. Then, just as she was thinking for what must have been the twentieth time that, dammit, she *would* call the desk, the door opened.

Jeff came in.

"What're you doing up?" he asked her.

"What'm *I* doing *up*? What're *you* doing out *there*? You had me scared silly."

"Sorry." He was breathing a little heavily. "I thought I heard someone fooling around with the car. Decided I'd better check. Then, when I went out, it was so damned dark. But as I shut the door behind me, it looked as if someone *was* there. Then I thought I heard running. I went in the direction of the sound."

"Why?" she asked, feeling the fear return again. Why would he have courted danger? After all, he was her husband, he was David's father; they needed him, depended on him . . .

Jeff shook his head. "You got me . . . Guess I was still half asleep. Sure made no sense, not these days. But it seemed like a really hot idea at the time. How long *you* been up?" he asked her.

"I don't know. A half hour. Maybe a little less. I had a nightmare. You were missing in it, too. I was—" She stopped herself, suddenly remembering about David, about what Jeff had been about to do to him. She couldn't tell that to him. "Well, it woke me up. And I found you *were* missing."

"A half hour or so," he muttered. "Guess you woke up just after I left."

She looked at him reproachfully. "You sure searched for a long time."

His breathing had eased, and he gave her a small smile. "Tell you the truth, after a while I found myself standing out there in the middle of nowhere, gulping in all that good air. And it just seemed so damned beautiful. The stars. The smell of the pines. I just stood there. Till I got cold." He smiled again, more widely this time. He stripped off his clothes and slid into the bed. "Come on, warm me up," he told her. Soon he had her forgetting the whole incident.

Chapter
8

Regret and anticipation mingled as they crossed the Delaware late the next afternoon and returned to New Jersey. Soon this wonderful weekend would be over. But there was David to see again, and home to return to. The morning and early afternoon had gone as beautifully as the day before; not once did she think of the dream or its aftermath.

The miles sped by, and soon they were only a few minutes from Peggy's. Still on the two-lane highway, they approached a motel that was coming up on their right. Frances' gaze was casual as she looked toward it. Then it sharpened. A car had stopped in front of one of the units. A man was getting out of it. It was Terrence.

The Roadside Rest. On Route 57. As they continued to drive, she found, not aware at first of what she was doing, that she was repeating it to herself, over and over again—*The Roadside Rest. Route* 57—as if to memorize it.

Consternation followed awareness. *Why? All of that's over.* She glanced at Jeff, his strong, dark profile unswervingly directed toward the road ahead. She cleared her throat. *I'll tell him now. Tell him all about Terrence. Get it out in the open, where it'll wither and die, once it's exposed to the light. We'll laugh at it, and I'll see it for the foolishness it is, the foolishness I already* know *it is. And then it'll be all over with. Done.*

But she found the words wouldn't come. Somehow she couldn't force them out. Or *wouldn't.*

Things didn't pick up any at Peggy's. When they walked into the house, David looked at them doubtfully. As if he didn't know who they were. He continued to regard them strangely while Peggy reported, "We've had a wonderful time. We were shooting owls under a blanket I rigged up, and made wonderful garages for David's cars out of the blocks he brought."

There was darkness around David's staring eyes. "How much sleep did he get?" Frances asked, sharpness in her voice. She knew from past experience that Peggy had no discipline when it came to getting David to bed. *That's what his reaction is all about,* she told herself angrily, uncertainly.

"Oh, I don't know. Maybe about one in the morning. There was a real good cowboy movie on."

What she said sparked something in David. "I'm a sheriff," he announced to no one in particular.

The Roadside Rest. The picture of the sign jumped into Frances' mind, almost as if triggered by David's declaration. She shook her head and gathered up her child, who made no protest, rested quiescently in her arms. "Peggy," she said, as they began to leave, "I really appreciate your taking care of him. We had a wonderful time. We needed to get away and it really helped. But please, please, the next time don't keep him up again. The last time he came down with an awful cold. Being so tired lowers his resistance . . ."

"Okay, okay," Peggy interrupted, cheerfully, dismissively. "The next time I'll be perfect. Just remember I'm here anytime you want me. David's my favorite man in the world. Just about," she added, and smiled up at Jeff with a glint in her eye that to Frances seemed mischievous.

Once in the car, David seemed to be himself again, acted as he always had with both of them, snuggling lovingly against Frances, squirming, chattering nonstop. More than once she kissed the top of his downy blond head. Her child. Her family. The three of them, going back to their home.

When they arrived, Jeff, always quicker than she—even though he first took the suitcases out of the backseat, having decided before they'd left the inn that there was no need to put them in the trunk—was up the stairs and onto the porch before she had David half out of the car.

Even before he had the door halfway open his curses exploded into the air.

Her heart sank. Whenever they left for a few days, she always had a mild uneasiness; a minor, unreasonable fear that when they returned, their home would be burned to the ground, or leveled by a storm. But there had been no storm, and there was no evidence of fire, either about the house or in the air. Had she left something running; the dishwasher, a faucet? Was the house flooded? Anxiously, pangs of guilt stabbing at her, she quickly followed Jeff in.

He was planted in the middle of the living room, raging. As she stared about her, her grip on David tightened.

The house had been ransacked, brutalized. Furniture was overturned, broken. An open can of black paint had been flung against one of the walls, soaking into the carpet beneath.

Jeff flew up the stairs. More curses, more slamming of doors. Frances remained where she'd halted, halfway through the doorway, immobilized. When Jeff came down, his face was livid. "It's the same up there," he spat out. "Everywhere."

In a daze, Frances stooped down, picked a ladder-back chair off the floor, set it upright and, David still in her arms, sat down in it. *The night I felt myself watched. The noises Jeff heard last night outside our room* . . .

Chapter
9

"TEENAGE KIDS."

That was what one of the detectives had told her when they arrived and surveyed what had happened. She'd grasped at the words as if they'd been a life preserver. *Teenage kids. That's all it was. Of* course. *Impulsive, stupid. Nothing premeditated. Nothing . . . threatening. All over with.*

Certainly, on second look, it appeared to have been mindless vandalism. So far as she and Jeff could tell, nothing had been taken. And little had been broken. A ladderback chair in the dining room, a mirror in their bedroom, a couple of David's small toys crushed, probably as they were stepped on. The living room wall was a mess, and the carpet unsalvageable. But Frances bought paint, and after three days and three coats, all applied during David's naps, the stain was blotted out. The rug had been old, and of poor quality—it had been one of their first purchases right after they'd married. Frances was glad to see it gone and replaced by their first really good rug: hand-loomed Turkish. *So some good came out of the whole thing,* she told herself. *And nothing really bad; nothing lasting.*

She had her hands full the first two weeks after the brief holiday. There was the house to restore, and then there was the matter of trying to restore Peggy. During the second week, her sister had another one of her down periods.

It seemed more caring to go to Peggy's, not to make her drive over, so for several days, after Peggy got home from work, she did that; took David with her, listened and made sympathetic noises or comments while David played or nestled against one of them.

"Sometimes I think he thinks *you're* his mother," Frances said one evening as David climbed up onto Peggy's lap.

"All the time I wish I were," came the answer.

Jeff was away again, and the three of them had had dinner together. It was dark now, long past David's bedtime. But she hadn't left because her sister had seemed so desperate to have her stay. Peggy couldn't get Martin off her mind, kept worrying it over and over. But now she seemed somewhat better, and besides, sister or no sister, it was time to go. Frances rose.

Peggy did, too, cradling a sleepy-looking David. "I really, truly appreciate all the time you've given me this week," she said, the tremulousness that had been in her voice for days no longer present. She continued jokingly, giving it a gravel edge, but Frances understood that she meant it: "You're the best Big Sister in the world."

It was just a six-mile drive to her own house, but the roads were narrow and winding and the maximum speed was only forty-five. It always took longer than it seemed it should.

After a few minutes Frances had the feeling that the car behind was following her, had turned each time she'd turned; hadn't turned where most cars would have.

Stop that, she told herself with asperity. *Nobody's following you. Everybody's got to be somewhere, don't they?* But it didn't do any good. She found herself making a left turn that would take her out of her way. The car behind followed. A quarter of a mile later she turned right, again out of her way. So did the car behind her.

"Why not? Why shouldn't it?" she muttered angrily to herself while David slept in the car seat behind her. But then tried slowing down, in the hope the car would pass her. It too slowed. *It's a narrow country road. I've probably got a farmer behind me. Farmers never care how slow they're going.* She chewed the inside of her lip. She knew why she was feeling this way. *Terrence.*

The damned weekend hadn't exorcised him at all. Even on that first terrible night—the night they'd returned to find their home violated—even on that night, when she'd gone to bed she found herself thinking of him. Of his sweetness, of the fragile beauty of the very little time they'd been able to share. She'd tried to fight it off, but despite herself, the longing had welled up in her heart, a feeling that had continued to plague her on almost a daily basis ever since. To be alone with him again. Just once . . .

They neared a main highway and she pulled onto it, swung the car abruptly to the left, away from the direction of her house. The lines of her mouth set.

Okay, if it's some kind of half-assed hysterical romanticism mixed up with just as half-assed guilt, let's spill it all out now, expose it to the light of day. She headed toward the Roadside Rest motel.

The decision absorbed her so completely she forgot about the car behind her. Minutes later, when she did finally glance up into the rearview mirror and saw headlights, it was meaningless. This was a busy road; it was likely someone would be behind her. And it didn't seem to matter anymore. Her feelings, whether paranoia, guilt, or even justified suspicion, had fled. There no longer was any sensation of being followed.

Realizing she was drawing closer, she began to think about turning back. *If I continue with this, I'm liable to make one huge fool of myself.* She shook her head. *Good. That's what you need.* She couldn't let this happen again. Couldn't let it happen to her, and to Jeff. And to David. Because, left within her, left to fester, it might in time affect them all, infect them all, destroy the entire family that Peggy so envied her for.

Then it hit her. *Of course.* Why hadn't she thought of it before? Because it was the perfect explanation. The reason she couldn't get Terrence out of her mind. Simple. So amusingly simple. No hysteria here at all. Wasn't she human? Didn't she need to know? To finally *know?* Find out what had happened. Why he had suddenly disappeared that one day in Brooklyn. *That's all this is. An unfinished mystery. Of course.* And then she did everything she could to concentrate on her driving and not think anymore. Just in case that weren't the reason.

Sooner than she'd expected it, the motel's sign loomed before her. Frances started to hit the brake hard, then remembered the cars behind her, and

David in the back. Instead she flicked the directional, slowed, and, missing the turnoff to the motel, rolled to a stop at the side of the road a hundred feet beyond it. *Another chance. The god of the total idiots has given you another chance to keep you from totally embarrassing yourself. When the cars behind all pass you, just hang a U; clear out of here.* But once the highway was free, she carefully began backing toward, and then into, the motel's driveway.

Parking at a distance from the motel office, she glanced back at David. He was asleep, and calm in that sleep, his body showing no signs of restlessness. *Better to leave him here.* If Terrence wasn't in, she'd be back almost immediately. And if he was, she'd go to the car first, take David with her before she knocked on Terrence's door.

Or—a second thought came to her—she'd stand at his door, watching the car while they spoke. Carefully, she checked to make sure all the wagon's doors were locked.

As she approached it, she saw the motel wasn't what she'd have expected of Terrence. Even in the muted light of the building, she could see paint flaking from its sides. When she opened the door to the office, there was a damp, musty aroma.

But of course he's only here temporarily. And what in this area is any better? Nothing that she knew of. Still . . .

An old woman, white-haired, deeply wrinkled, looked up from behind the desk. Her small blue eyes were very sharp.

"I'm looking for Mr. Horgan. Terrence Horgan."

The clerk stared at her flintily. After a moment she consulted a book. "Room one-two-one. At the far end.

To your left." Her voice was like scrapings on a black-board.

The woman, her back already toward her, hadn't said if he was in, and Frances didn't ask. She probably wouldn't know. More important, she was anxious to get away from the woman's penetrating eyes. Leaving the office, she hurried to the room. Passing the station wagon, she didn't think to look inside.

Even before she reached Terrence's room, Frances saw there was no light coming from his window. She knocked on the door, waited, then knocked again. For the first time she became aware of the rate of her heart, of her difficulty in breathing. *Like I used to get before our dates.*

She knocked a third time. There was no response. With her shoulders hunched and her head lowered she slowly walked back toward the car. It wasn't until she was halfway there that she realized she'd never once planned what she was going to say to Terrence. It had never occurred to her that her presence there would have to be explained. *What would I have told him? What could I have said without embarrassing myself? That I needed the "mystery" solved? At this hour, what would he have thought of me? What would he have expected of me?*

Maybe she would even have given him false hope, she thought. *False.*

As she opened the door to the wagon, she heard David's soft crying. The overhead light had gone on, and she turned and saw the tears coursing down his frightened face. "You left me alone. You left me all alone in the car!" he sobbed. "In the *dark*!"

Instantly, insanely, the image returned: David's running to Jeff, crying, "A man from the bakery talked to Mommy!'' Would he scream this out, too? Frantically, Frances reached over, pulled him out of the car seat and held him. "Mommy was just gone for a second. I was nearby all the time."

He couldn't be mollified. She held him, crooned to him, but his sobs wouldn't stop, and he squirmed in her arms unhappily, distrustfully. She felt the need to drive away. *Now.* Before Terrence arrived, before his headlights fell on her, picked her out, *revealed* her.

But no one came. Then finally, finally David was all right, falling asleep in the middle of a soft, sighing sob. Carefully, gently, she lifted him back into his little cushioned seat, made sure he was comfortable. She turned the ignition key and quietly wheeled the wagon out of the lot.

An idea came to her. Jeff wasn't expected back till late that night. She'd stop by Peggy's first. This time she'd air it all out. Spill every last bit of it, everything she had to say about Terrence. Talk for hours if she had to, go on and on until she got it all out of her system.

Almost immediately Frances felt better, became almost calm. It would be a change; *her* talking, *Peggy* listening, sympathizing, advising if asked. She was sure Peggy would welcome it, would be happy to reciprocate, to be, for the first time in how long, the shoulder cried upon. *And I respect Peggy's judgment. So long as it doesn't have to do with her choice in men*, she added to herself. Peggy's men had never exactly been total disasters, but right from the beginning, even when she was a kid, she'd seemed to have this fatal attraction to guys who were at least some shade of wrongo . . . culminating, of course, in the most questionable of them all, Martin.

The miles fell away, and finally she was back on Peggy's small, unlit street. She drew near the house, and then very nearly continued to drive straight on past it; instantly confused, frightened, uncertain.

Jeff's car was in Peggy's driveway.

Chapter
10

THEY WERE HAVING AN AFFAIR. OF COURSE. WHY HADN'T she seen it before? Peggy's mischievous smile as she'd said "David's my favorite man in the world. Just about." *And it's your own damned fault. You had to whine that things weren't perfect between you and Jeff. So she could tell herself she wasn't really hurting anyone, not breaking anything that wasn't already broken.*

Furiously, Frances shook her head. *Stop making yourself miserable.* There's a logical answer to all of this. *Stuff all the melodramatic garbage, and go say hello to your sister and husband.* She reached back and lifted an unprotesting David out of his car seat. His eyes opened for an instant, and then closed again, a small smile forming on his lips as if to say that it was okay now, that he felt safe again.

Less than an hour before, Peggy had been dressed in slacks and a blouse. Now when she opened the door she was in a light robe. *But of course she would be. It's nearly time for bed.* Peggy was blinking at her, startled.

In that first instant Frances was afraid Peggy was going to ask her why she was there, why she'd come back, and for the second time that night Frances realized she had no speech prepared. But instead Peggy said, "I was going to sack out and watch TV . . ." Her voice was a little shaky as she added, "and then Jeff turned up."

Frances nodded, and walked into the hall.

"His car broke down on the way home. He was able to nurse it here," Peggy finished.

"So he's here now?" Frances asked as they moved into the small living room. She'd yet to see a sign of Jeff.

"Yes," Peggy, still behind her, said. And then as she came into the room and appeared to look around, "I mean, he *was* here. He's walked over to the garage to see what they can do for him." Was her voice unnecessarily loud? Frances wondered. As if she were giving instructions?

"Kind of a long walk," Frances said tersely. She'd seen Peggy's car parked in the driveway. A car Jeff could have borrowed.

"Yeah. But he said it was no problem. You know, the usual thing with him. Like always, said he could use the exercise." Peggy walked halfway out of the room into the kitchen, then back. Had she been looking for Jeff in there? Or was he upstairs, in Peggy's bedroom? At the same time, both sisters glanced in that direction. "You want something to drink or anything?" Peggy asked. "He might be a while."

They had coffee and waited. Peggy had the living room TV on. Once she'd seated herself, she stared at it relentlessly, all of her conversation directed only toward what was happening on the screen. Frances,

David still in her arms, saw nothing as she stared at the set. Instead she pictured Jeff returning, perhaps not seeing her car—she'd parked it across the street, in the unlit shadows. He'd walk in totally unaware, see her, gasp, and then, in a rush of words, tell her, get it all off his chest, let her know that their marriage was over, finished, had been a joke right from the start. And that he planned to fight her with everything he had—for David.

She closed her eyes, pressed them hard. She couldn't believe what she'd come to. *You're out of it. Everything you're thinking is absolutely out of it. Bonkers City. Of course Jeff's car is here. It broke down. Cars break down. And cars can be nursed. Remember the time with our first car when one of the valves, or whatever it was, went? Remember how many miles we were able to go, limping all the way? And of course he didn't use Peggy's car; he doesn't like to borrow cars, ever since that accident with a friend's convertible when he was a kid. And you know he does get a little concerned about his not exercising enough. The long flight from Texas; he was probably stiff, wanted to work out the kinks. That's all this is.*

She opened her eyes, glanced over at her sister. *And of course Peggy is staring at the screen, not looking at you, not getting into any kind of conversation. Hadn't she planned to catch a little TV? After a week, aren't the two of us talked out anyway? For God's sake, give her some credit. She's a moral person. You know that. She wouldn't steal Jeff away.* And then Frances remembered again about Peggy's choices in men, all the times her usual good judgment had foundered, and always each time with a man.

Nearly an hour went by. Then, very suddenly, Jeff

arrived. He didn't knock, simply burst the front door open, walked briskly through the foyer, into the living room . . . and saw Frances. His mouth dropped, his gaze flicked toward Peggy and then back to Frances.

"Babe! What a break! Did Peggy tell you about the car?"

His voice was expansive, his expression innocent. *Very* expansive. *Very* innocent. Frances gave him a small smile for an answer.

"Great," he said, still as expansive, still as innocent-eyed, "because they're going to have to tow the thing tomorrow morning. Too late tonight. So I won't have to bother you after all," he smiled, turning to Peggy. Her face was a mask.

Chapter
11

LIFE'S NEVER WHOLLY WHAT IT SEEMS, NO MATTER what's going on, Frances found herself thinking the next morning as she trundled a cart through Shop-Rite. Even in the midst of the abnormal, normal things went on. Had to. People had to eat, sleep, re-lieve themselves, wash clothes, shop.

She'd even hoped that coming here, going through all the old familiar motions, might help. At first she even tried to force herself to listen intently to the dopey mood music piped throughout the store, had hoped its honey and sappiness would soothe and calm her, normalize her life. But finally she'd given up. No matter how hard she tried to force herself, within a few moments she'd find herself back in the middle of the storm. The storm she kept attempting to convince herself was wholly of her own making.

Even David's continuous stream of chatter was lost on her; those few times when he insistently called her attention to something, her focus on what he was say-ing came slowly, blurrily, as if she were coming out of a coma.

Frances found herself going over the arguments again and again, foolishly, obsessively, fruitlessly. *It's all a crock, this stewing. He wasn't that far out of his way, coming from Newark, and it was natural he'd try to get to Peggy's. He feels comfortable with her, likes her, respects her. So naturally he'd try to get there if he could, and figure she'd know a reasonably trustworthy mechanic.*

And yet . . . And yet . . . And here it always began all over again.

Peggy is a woman without a husband. Peggy is a good person, a moral person. But morality stretches just so far when you're desperate. When you're starving, you steal bread. When you're achingly lonely, emotionally starved, sexually frustrated . . .

As she reached out for a package of Oreos—David's favorite—it came to her. An entirely new thought, one that froze her in mid-motion.

Maybe Martin didn't disappear.

For a moment everything about her—the things on the shelves, the other customers, the music, became very sharp, very clear, *heightened.*

Maybe this has nothing at all to do with the moaning I did to Peggy about Jeff. Because maybe this isn't something new. Maybe this has been a long-term affair. You've heard about married men who have affairs with their sisters-in-law. Hell, you've even known a couple of people it happened to. And maybe somewhere along the line Martin found out. And he attacked them when he found out, and they killed him—or killed him before *he found out.*

Well, that was some thought, wasn't it? *Nice going, Frances. I'd love to read what you're going to write about How I Spent My Summer.*

It couldn't be true. If it were, would Peggy have been so periodically distraught ever since? *Or has it all been a cover-up? A way of getting comfort and sympathy and companionship for the guilt she was feeling, not because of a broken heart, or loneliness or uncertainty?*

Frances blinked. *Back on that road again. Already. I'm really amazing myself. How about thinking about something normal for a change? How about thinking of, let's see . . . cereal?* she told herself with a sarcasm she hoped would purge all the idiocy. She gave the cart a purposeful push.

There were a few people ahead of her in the checkout line. She'd bought David a small toy, and, seated in the cart, he was absorbed by it, fondled it, stared at it through the blister pack that still encased it.

As usual, she had the paper with her. On the bottom right hand of the front page there was a feature story about the two local murder cases. She started to flip the page, with a rapidity not normal to her. And then turned back and began to read. For no reason that she could fathom, she found herself *drawn.*

Whoever had written the story—there was no byline —seemed to be sure a serial killer was involved. Each girl had been found strangled, each had been stripped naked, with none of their clothes yet found. Both had had a simple gold chain about the neck. Yet in the first case, at least, no one had yet remembered the victim owning that particular kind of jewelry, and in the second there was some uncertainty.

More important, according to the account, there was no known link between the women apart from that of geography. Each had attended different schools, each worked in a different area. They had no mutual friends. One was in her mid-twenties, the second in her early thirties. One had been a blonde, the other a redhead. The younger one had been slender. The redhead had been voluptuous, in fact at one time had modeled for bathing suits.

So far, the report continued, the police appeared to have made no progress on the cases. There had been no sightings of strange men or cars, either before or after. No fingerprints had been found, and nothing yet had been discovered that seemed to furnish a clue.

The story concluded with comments by the victims' relatives and friends, determined quotes by officials working on the case, and interviews with young women in the area, all of the latter professing to be frightened and taking precautions.

"Miss. *Miss.*"

Frances, startled, looked up from the paper. There was no longer a line in front of her. Flustered, she hurried to unload her groceries. *Next thing you know, you'll be reading the supermarket tabloids*, she told herself, sickened and puzzled by how thoroughly she'd been drawn into the kind of sordid thing she usually avoided.

She was halfway to her car, still railing at herself, when she saw him. He was leaning against it.

Terrence.

"Saw you through the window. At the checkout counter," he told her as she stopped in front of him. He pointed toward his watch. "Figured I'd invite you to lunch." There was grace in the way he stood, and the light in his eyes was vibrant, *alive*.

Stunned, barely able to think, Frances started to protest, but he gently stopped her. "Please. I owe it to you. I was too poor back then to treat you to much of anything. It's time I spent something on you."

Time seemed to hang suspended as she looked at him, his crisp auburn hair ruffling slightly in the summer breeze, his gaze expectant, his smile warm and unthreatening. She glanced at David, thought of Jeff. And Peggy. *I need to be alone, to nurse my wounds, to get over this insane suspicion of mine*, she protested to herself, and then said "All right."

It took a few moments for him to help her unload the groceries into the car. Once she began walking toward the restaurant with him, David toddling along at her side, Frances was astonished to find herself feeling sixteen again, free of all responsibility, of all ties. Yet, oddly, she suddenly realized, life at that moment felt more real to her than it had in years.

Back in her bathroom, Frances looked into the mirror to see if any of it showed on her face. It seemed impossible that it wouldn't, but several moments of scrutiny indicated nothing had changed. She turned away, uncertain as to whether she was relieved or disappointed.

David had been impossible since they'd returned home. In the car he'd been no problem; in fact, she realized now, a chill stealing over her, he'd been as quiet in the car as he had the time she'd cruised the mall, looking for Terrence. Her eyes went back to the bathroom mirror: the look they returned was wide, wild, frightened. *He doesn't know anything. He's too young to understand.*

To her shame, she found herself remembering her reaction to his crankiness when they returned home; her suppressed rage, an anger far too deep to be a normal reaction. *Perhaps, unconsciously, I was already afraid he'd understood?* She sank onto the edge of the tub. *For God's sake, don't do this to him. Don't take your guilt—your madness—out on him.* And then a thought struck her. Quickly she rose and walked into her bedroom. There she strode purposefully to Jeff's desk.

He had a calendar there, a five-year calendar, on which he kept notes; business, personal. Comings and goings, meetings, vacations . . . She began to flick the pages backward, back to the time when Martin had disappeared. To see where Jeff had been that day . . .

But she stopped before she got to it, sickened.

He's your husband. You love him. He loves you. Stop. Stop all of this. Stop this game, this stupid game . . .

And then, sighing, she fell into the chintz-covered chair. *Terrence.* Her body relaxed, softened, her arms fell away from her body, rested alongside it, palms upturned.

Throughout their brief lunch she'd felt as if she were floating. It was only a small, not terribly clean pizzeria, but somehow that felt more right than if it had been the finest of restaurants; it was the kind of place they might have gone to together, all those years before.

She hadn't noticed, not for a moment, what she was eating; wasn't even sure now that she had eaten anything at all. Terrence had taken only a few bites, and then stopped. It came back to her then—their one meal together, coming out of Prospect Park on a sunfilled afternoon. He'd ordered a hamburger then, and had barely nibbled at it . . . too smitten to think about food. Had instead gazed into her eyes intently, longingly . . . just as he had today.

Incredibly, the innocence about him then still seemed to be there. *No, not* innocence, *really,* she corrected herself. *A purity.* He'd understood the world then, just as he understood it now. But he'd been uncorrupted then—even at that age it had been a far from usual thing—and he seemed to be the same way now. Wiser, of course, knocked around a bit, but still essentially what he'd been—a good, decent, kind human being, the kind who made society better, not worse. A man with a sense of perspective, and a correspondingly perceptive humor. And one who looked at her in a way no other man ever had.

"Why did you disappear like that? So suddenly? Without ever calling me? Or writing?" she'd finally worked up the courage to ask.

The pain that crossed his face took her back sixteen years; made her see the pain he'd felt then. "My father was transferred from his job. Just like that. To the state of Washington. Those were the days when, if your company wanted to move you, you didn't argue with them.

"I suppose he must have had some advance warning, but no one told me anything. Not till I came home from school that day. I went straight to the airport with my mother, flew to Washington. My father followed the next day, driving along behind all the furniture."

She'd only looked at him, waiting, not wanting to ask again.

And he seemed to understand. He'd looked away, chewed at his lip, then told her. "Washington. All the way across the continent. I should have written you, I suppose, but I couldn't. It was as if, in just minutes, my whole life, the only part of it that meant anything to me, had been taken away. I was devastated. I had no money. I was three thousand miles away from you and knew it'd be years before I could ever go back." He looked away then, and his smile became wry. "And of course," he went on, "I was also a kid. Just a dumb kid."

"You were never dumb," she told him softly, remembering how proud she'd been of him in school; he'd been the top student in the classes they'd shared, but not in the way most of the brains in her school had been—stodgy and unimaginative.

The papers he'd written in English had had originality and flair. He'd even managed to make geometry —*geometry,* of all things—amusing. His answers, always correct, were often interlaced with humor, a dry, quiet humor that had made even the teacher laugh. Those had been their only classes together. Sometimes she'd cut one of her own to be with him during his free period.

He shook his head. "No, I *was* dumb," he repeated. "But not dumb enough to forget you. I never did that."

The pause after he said that had been awkward, and she'd used the pretext of getting David home to break the mood. Now she leaned back in the chair and allowed herself to recapture all the feelings she'd had as they'd walked back to the car. Neither of them speaking, just as when they'd been young; just being together then had been enough. And again it had been today. But this time she'd yearned for his arm about her, and she'd been sure he felt the same way.

But of course she wouldn't have allowed it. It was

enough, she'd told herself then, and now told herself again, that she'd had this. This would be enough to last her a lifetime. Would *have* to be, she assured herself grimly.

Terrence had offered her the opportunity to see him again. "I hope we can have another lunch," he'd begun, but she'd quickly shaken her head, cutting him off.

"All right," he'd said, and nodded, for the first time not looking at her. "But if someday, somehow, we bump into each other again, then maybe . . ."

She hadn't replied, had got into the car, her eyes lowered, fighting back what might have become tears.

Chapter
12

W<small>HEN JEFF CAME HOME THAT NIGHT, HE ASKED FRANCES</small>
how lunch had gone.

She wheeled away from him instantly, reflexively, her face burning, her eyes gone wide. She pretended to busy herself at a drawer. "What do you mean?" she asked.

"Called you a few times around lunch," he replied, his voice seemingly casual. "When you didn't answer, the brilliant, detectivelike part of my brain went into action; deduced that you'd decided to have lunch out. Have anything good?"

Detective. Why had he used that word? Was it on his mind? Had he hired a detective, hoping to catch her with someone so that he could divorce her, gain custody of David? *No. That makes no sense at all. It's just your guilt speaking.* But when she turned and answered, she found herself studying him, watching his response.

I had lunch with Terrence. Remember? That old boyfriend of mine I was so gaga about? You know, from junior year in high school? Well, he's moved into the area and we've run into each other a couple of times. When he invited me to lunch, I figured why not?

Perfectly harmless, all of it. Nothing he could become upset by, not really. It was what she wanted to tell him, what she'd thought she decided to tell him. But instead she heard herself saying, "I went shopping late. Decided to go to the pizza place at Jamesway."

"Just you and David?"

She stared at him. "Yes. Just me and David."

Jeff nodded. "It must have been nice for the two of you. You probably should get out more." Then he turned and left the room.

She remained rooted for some moments, staring after him, shaken. *He doesn't suspect,* she told herself over and over again. But it didn't help. *Need to talk to someone.* She walked to the phone. *Peggy. Who else is there?* She'd set a time for drinks that night. *After all,* she told herself wryly, *didn't Jeff just tell me I should get out more?*

The place Peggy had suggested was a mistake. Frances realized it the moment she stepped into the small bar and restaurant. Its look was dingy; cheap paneling on the walls, grungy-looking tables, mottled wooden floors. It didn't help any that the people at the bar, unintelligent-looking, dirty-looking, sloppily dressed, were discussing what seemed to be a third murder in the area.

Deliberately she found a table farthest from the talk and waited for her sister, waited till she arrived before ordering her drink. When the waitress, trying to be chatty, began speaking about the third strangled woman, Frances cut her off.

She had enough on her mind, needed to shred the

last remnants of her suspicion about Jeff and Peggy before her sister arrived. She had about convinced herself when Peggy came in. But not quite. Frances found herself scrutinizing her sister as she had Jeff short hours before. Was there a tightness to her face, an uncertainty in her eyes? *And if so, so what? There could be a million reasons for her looking like that.*

The waitress wandered over. They ordered their drinks; a vodka collins for Peggy, vodka and tonic for herself. Peggy didn't seem to be feeling well. When asked, she said, "Splitting headache all day." *A headache from guilt?* Frances was appalled to find herself thinking. Then Peggy asked her, "Okay, what's up?" Her voice and expression were dispassionate.

Frances found herself stumbling through the recital; trying to confine it only to Terrence and her feelings toward him, the whole absurd muddle she'd got herself into, this insane, well, almost *obsession* . . . But at the same time she had to steer clear of the other thoughts that kept threatening to intrude themselves into her speech . . . her suspicions about Peggy, about Jeff, about Martin's disappearance . . . Because sometimes what she was saying about Terrence began to lead into those other things, those wild, sick, destructive suspicions . . .

So she kept stumbling, and the more she spoke, the less satisfactory it became. What made it worse was that Peggy seemed odd, removed; the way she'd been at her house the night Jeff said he'd broken down. There were none of the usual empathetic nods, the appropriate responses. In fact no responses at all; none that meant anything. Eventually Frances began to drift, somehow got onto the subject of Martin.

Halfway through, she noticed the grimness in

Peggy's expression. It bewildered her, added to the uneasiness she'd felt all evening with her sister. "Have I said something wrong?" she faltered.

Peggy stared at her. Silently. When she finally began to speak, her voice was cold. "I can't believe you," she said. "The girl with everything. Turning it into nothing."

Frances went numb, became frozen. It came at her that hard.

"There you sit, complaining about a guy like Jeff, pushing yourself further and further into something you may not ever be able to get out of. All for a phantom; some guy you dated a few times when life was easy, and we all walked around with stars in our eyes. And here I am, left with nothing but memories of a no-good."

Her voice was growing harsh, and the alcohol—she had had two drinks—seemed to be slurring her speech.

Frances, unsettled to begin with, and now stricken by Peggy's reaction, told her, "I'm sorry. You're right. I shouldn't have bothered you with this."

"*Sorry*?" Peggy's voice was a sneer. "A lot you've got to be sorry about. A husband like Jeff. A guy like Terrence still carrying the torch for you. All those other boyfriends you had: the cream of the crop. God, if I'd had even one . . ." She drew a breath. "Mooning over Terrence when you've got a husband most women would kill for . . . *I'd* kill for. All that prattle last time about his faults. Listen, if all he had was those faults and nothing but, he'd still be plenty all right with me." Her voice had risen to the point where people were beginning to stare. Frances gently tried to hush her.

Peggy's eyes flared. "Who the hell cares about my voice? Who in Christ is ever going to *hear* it? I swear to God, Frances, I have half a mind to tell Jeff all about your crap with Terrence—he's always thought of you as some kind of half-baked saint. Like to see his face when he hears about all your little fantasies . . . Like to, but I won't. Because *him* I don't want to hurt!"

She rose unsteadily. "And David. Goddamn you. You've gotta have David, *too*. And what do I have? What the hell do *I* have? *You*. For a sister." With that she left the restaurant.

The waitress was discreet, overly, awkwardly discreet when a stunned Frances fumbled through her bag, trying to gather up the money for the check as quickly as she could. She felt humiliated, crushed, kept her head down as she exited, sure that everyone in the place was staring at her.

Outside, in the car, she sat for a long time, alone in the dark, crying. *What's happening to me? What's happening to my perfect little world?* Just a few weeks before it had all seemed so sure, so safe, so *right*.

Finally, exhausted, she started the car, automatically punched the radio on.

A station, probably one of those distant ones that faded in and out here in the country evenings, was playing the kind of music that had been popular in the 1930s, the kind of songs she tried to avoid listening to whenever she was alone, because of their power to inevitably, invariably sadden her, demoralize her. But this time she made no move to change the station, to turn the radio off.

In time, as she drove, the station faded away, and the local one from near her home took over. Oddly, they were playing the same kind of music: usually it was nothing but country and rock. She felt the tears come again, and let them.

A half mile from the house the news report came on. It was about the murder. "Her decomposing body—" the announcer said before she violently snapped the radio off.

She'd planned to sit in the car until she got control of herself, wipe away the tears, make herself presentable. Instead, as she reached the house, she tightened, then jumped out of the wagon as soon as it stopped. Jeff's car wasn't in the driveway. And he was supposed to be home minding David.

Did Peggy call him? Has he already left me? Taken David with him? Real fear took hold of her. She raced up the steps and into the house.

She called softly to Jeff as she entered, just in case, but there was no answer. Only the dining room light was on, the one light they'd leave on when they left the house at night. Quickly she ran to the stairs and up them. No light in their room, she noticed, and flew to David's. His door was closed.

Quietly, anxiously, she pulled it open. The light from the hall filtered in. She felt her knees give way. He was all right. He was in his bed asleep, his covers gently rising and falling as he breathed.

Relief welling up in her, Frances went to her son, her only child, reached down to touch his cheek—and stopped. Her hand was shaking so much she knew there was no way she could control it. Instead she withdrew it, looked at him for another moment, then left the room, went downstairs to look for a note from Jeff.

She found none.

Back upstairs she checked their bedroom, even the

bathroom. But there was nothing, no slip of paper with hurried writing. *Call Peggy*, the impulse came, but she dismissed it, unwilling to be humiliated by her a second time. Because whether or not Jeff was with her, there'd still be humiliation. Instead Frances sank into the small chintz-covered chair and waited. She sat for an hour, two . . . Then, despite herself, she felt sleep begin to take hold of her. Three times her head nodded, dropped, then jerked back sharply. Finally she succumbed. Fully clothed, she stretched out on the bed and instantly fell asleep.

Chapter
13

THE SKY WAS JUST BEGINNING TO LIGHTEN WHEN FRANCES awakened. Immediately she became aware she was still alone in the bed. Her heart sank. Maybe something had happened to Jeff. Some kind of an abduction. It seemed preposterous, but in a world like this, anything was possible.

To have been entrusted with David, and to have left the house on his own . . . Okay, sometimes he could be a little irresponsible, but not to have returned by morning . . . All at once she felt a loss that was both formless and terrible. It took her a few moments to figure out what it was, but finally it came to her. *Jeff's solidity*. She'd never before realized how much she depended on it.

It was a trait of his she'd never even thought about. But . . . *solid* . . . someone with strength she could lean on. That's what he had. That's who he was. Even physically he was that way. Big-bodied, full-muscled. When she placed a hand upon his shoulder, it would feel as if she were resting it on a boulder. There was no give to it at all; just solidity, firm, reassuring solidity. What he was spiritually as well as physically.

Now all of that might be gone.

And maybe, just maybe, he was gone because of this self-indulgent game she'd been playing with herself. Capricious fantasies about a boy she'd barely known. To destroy her marriage, wreck her family, for that . . .

Still lying on the bed, she lifted her head. She'd thought she heard a noise, a sound of movement. Her body beginning to tense, she strained to hear more. There was no sound, but for the first time she noticed something else . . . a faint aroma. It seemed to be coffee.

Quickly she arose. She peered toward the clock; just past five. Leaving her room, she glanced toward David's door. It was still closed. For an instant she turned toward it, hesitated, and then stopped herself. No need to check on him. *Of* course *he's all right.* Reaching the stairs, she slowly, quietly, made her way down them. There was still no sound, but there was no question now; it *was* coffee she was smelling.

At the bottom of the stairs she stopped. From here she couldn't see into the kitchen. "Jeff?" she asked quietly.

There was no answer.

She tried again, louder this time, feeling herself begin to shake, telling herself there was nothing to worry about.

"Frances." There was a stir, and then he came through the kitchen door. It was Jeff, tousled-looking, in business shirt and pants, his tie and collar loosened.

Relief clashed with anger and a sense of betrayal.

"Where have you been?" she implored, her lowered voice harsh with emotion. "How could you have left David like that?"

What appeared to be genuine contrition pulled at Jeff's face. "I know, I know. I'm sorry, Frances, I really am. We had a terrible emergency at work. A huge cave-in on that Texas project. The company could lose hundreds of thousands—maybe even more if there are any screwups with the reinsurance. Doughty called last night and insisted I get into the office and monitor the whole thing, go over all the contracts."

He shook his head wearily. "I'd forgotten where you and Peggy were meeting. And I felt so pressured, I forgot to leave you a note. Then when I got to the office, I didn't want to call, afraid I might wake you up. I just got back a few minutes ago."

"But David—" she began, still unable to understand how he could have left him.

"I know," he told her, again looking contrite, even ashamed. "But it was one of those bang-bang things— I had to get out right away, and I was sure you'd be home any minute. Till then I knew he'd be safe. Nothing was going to happen. Not out here."

"Not out *here*? Not after what happened to our *house* while we were *gone*?"

He shrugged. "One in a million."

She sank onto the nearest chair, feeling as if it had all become too much for her. It had been insane of Jeff to have left David like that, and yet she knew, logically, that he was right. The odds against anything having happened were astronomical. And of course nothing *did* happen. And men, unlike women, had not been born with, or inculcated with, a nurturing instinct.

Jeff came to her, knelt before her. "I'm sorry," he said, looking up into her eyes. "I didn't mean to upset you like this. I guess maybe I panicked when Doughty called. I mean, if things were going better for me at work, if I wasn't the guy who'd written the contract on this . . ."

All his solidity had vanished. He looked like a contrite, frightened little boy. She softened, reached out to him, plunged her hand into his thick mat of hair, caressed it. "I know. I know. But mothers can be funny people." Her hand stopped, and she looked at him directly. "Wives, too."

It was time to tell him. Get it all out, get it over with. Finally. And then they could start fresh, no longer encumbered by her schoolgirl whims. "You know, when I said I just had lunch with David . . ." she began.

He stared at her blankly.

"When you asked me if I'd had lunch out. And I said I had. And you asked me who I'd had it with. And I said just David."

He nodded slowly, as if only dimly remembering. As if because to him it had been so inessential, inconsequential . . .

"Well, I did have lunch with someone else. I mean, David and I did," she added, not to make it sound any worse than it was.

"Do you remember Terrence? That boy I told you about falling in love with when I was in high school?"

Jeff's eyes began to search her.

"Well, I had lunch with him."

She told him all of it then; told him all of the facts, some of her fantasies; leaving out her conjectures about him and Peggy and Martin; all the nightmarish thoughts. "I don't know why I got so caught up," she concluded. "Maybe it was just unfinished business. You know, being cut off so abruptly like that. So maybe it was just something I had to resolve. Debris of the past that had to be cleared away. So I could get on with my life. *Our* life."

Jeff rose slowly, a little stiffly. He'd listened calmly, patiently, attentively, not once interrupting her or joking, as he often did. His gaze had never left her, was in fact still on her. He nodded. His expression was thoughtful, serious. "Sure," he said finally. "That's what it sounds like to me. I don't blame you. It was another time. There was no reality to it. No diapers to change, no toilet bowls to scrub . . ."

To her astonishment, as his reasonable words came at her, she felt anger flash. As if somehow he shouldn't have been that understanding, shouldn't have shrugged it off so lightly, so easily.

But then David called. By the time she had him out of bed and got breakfast going, her rancor had subsided. It seemed to disappear entirely as she listened sympathetically to Jeff's tale of the crisis at work; it was a truly desperate one, from the way he described it. Despite having had no sleep, he felt he had to go back in. After showering, shaving, and dressing, he left at the usual time.

An hour and a half after he'd gone, the phone rang and she picked it up. It was Charlie Bergman, a co-worker of Jeff's. Frances had met him at one or two of the office's parties. Jeff liked him, and she had, too. He was a quiet man, and his eyes had been complicitly humorous. "Is Jeff there?" he asked after a few pleasantries.

For a moment she didn't quite understand. How

could he be here when he was at work? "No. He left here at the usual time. He should be there by now."

Bergman sighed. "Ah well, must have got caught in traffic. Thanks."

As he started to hang up, she lightly interjected, "Anyway, it's okay if he's late. I mean, since you guys kept him there so late last night."

There was silence on the other end of the phone. And then, "Oh. Yeah, right. Thanks again."

After he hung up, she stood there for a long time with the receiver still in her hand. Finally, she walked into the kitchen and tried to distract herself with the newspaper.

The story of the newest murder was spread across the whole top of the front page. She stared numbly at it, tried to concentrate on it, but the words ran together, made no sense. Once, twice, three times she tried to read the opening paragraph, but finally gave up.

There was a state forest a few miles from their home. It was a beautiful day. She'd take David there. It was a place where she could clear her mind, lose this numbing suspicion that had taken hold of her since Charlie Bergman's last words.

It wasn't till they were on their way that Frances realized the drive would take her directly past Terrence's motel.

Chapter 14

JESUS CHRIST. FRANCES STARED OUT OF HER KITCHEN window the next morning. Jeff had just kissed her good-bye and left for work. He'd said nothing at all about being late for work the previous day, and she hadn't asked him. She also hadn't told him, found she hadn't been able to bring herself to tell him, about Charlie Bergman's call. No matter how she'd said it to him, how she'd presented it, *she* at least would have known she was being distrustful, prying. And a marriage couldn't survive that kind of thing.

She had to get over all of that. The disgust had filled her again, the disgust that had come with knowingly driving past the motel only hours after she'd told Jeff all about it, after letting him know it had been nothing in the first place and was all over now, words she had believed as she'd said them. Driving past, she'd deliberately not looked over at the motel, had kept her eyes fastened on the road.

But she hadn't deceived herself.

Mrs. Emenesky. Dammit, if only we were friends. Even an old lady like that, Frances thought desperately, feeling a terrible need to unburden herself, tell it all to someone, someone to whom she *could* tell all of it, even to the very last of her sickest imaginings. *If only there were someone I'd become friends with here. Had regular get-togethers over coffee with, talked together the way women do, or used to, before everybody thought she had to have a goddamn career.* Of the three other women scattered along their mile and a half of road, two worked, and the other was in her eighties, even older than Mrs. Emenesky.

Frances turned away from the window, lifted David out of his high chair, cleaned off his face, took him into his little playroom and sat there with him, for once not busying herself with anything as she watched him.

Peggy. Again she saw her sister's flushed, angry face. She had never known, not really, how jealous Peggy had been of her. Had thought that all had vanished after their teenage years. They'd been so close once she and Peggy had got out into the world. *And of course even more so, after Martin disappeared.* The room was too hot, and she stood and opened all the windows, but it didn't seem to help. She sat again, still thinking of Peggy. *I've been a good sister to her. I know I have. And she's been one to me. I love her. And she loves me. I'm sure of that,* she told herself fiercely, trying to force a certainty that, despite all the ferocity, wouldn't quite come.

She thought of calling Peggy at work, but found she couldn't. It was too soon. The wounds were still too new, too raw.

David had been playing near her feet, happily absorbed with two G.I. Joes Jeff had recently bought him. But now he glanced up and reached toward her.

She pulled him onto her lap and asked, "Would you like me to read to you?"

"Ragamuffin Puppy," he said, nodding happily.

She found the little book about the Ragamuffin Puppy, and David nestled contentedly against her. She thought he probably liked the book as much for its name as anything. He took particular relish in pronouncing "Ragamuffin."

But today, after a few moments, the book didn't seem to hold him. He squirmed, looked uninterested, got up and down a couple of times, then finally put his hand on the pages. "No more," he said decisively, slid off her lap and resumed playing with his G.I. Joes. It was the first time he'd ever done that.

Had this been any other time, she'd have smiled to herself, proud that at this young age, David was already asserting his independence. But now she felt hurt. And even, she realized guiltily, resentful. Resentment was a form of hostility. And to feel hostility, no matter how slightly, toward her wonderful little boy, her bright, good-hearted, adorable little boy . . .

Therapy. Maybe that's what I need. A psychiatrist. Immediately she canceled out any hope of that. Not now. Money was tight enough as it was. Not with Jeff feeling as shaky about his career as he was . . .

David continued to play at her feet as she remained stiffly seated in the chair, the corners of her mouth working while she tried to sort it all out, take care of it all by herself. *It's so foolish. Nobody's that wonderful. If Terrence is so damned terrific, why did his marriage fall apart?*

Oh sure. Because he was hoping she was just like me. What a crock. She pushed at the vulgarity of the last words, as if somehow that would bring the whole damn fantasy down to earth.

The way something else had come down to earth. *Jeff.* All the little cracks, the fissures, the things she'd ignored, patched up, pretended didn't exist. Her marriage had been perfect. *Had* to be. So she'd ignored the slights, the cruelties, glossed them over. His casual brutalities. The times he'd gotten nasty with waitresses. The man in the bar he got into that fight with. Jeff pounding his fist into the man's head, over and over again . . . She'd pushed all of that away, excused it, pretended it had never happened. Told no one. Because that would have let in the light of day. Exposed it all. Demolished perfection.

Because it had had to be perfect. When it wasn't, you made it perfect anyway, saw only the good. Ignored the rest. Because of Mom. Because of the way she'd seen life. Because of how she'd remembered Dad.

There was only one way that life could be. It had to be ideal. Otherwise it was nothing. It was what Mom had believed. *It was what she made me believe, too.* Of course, all the good things had been long before, times she barely remembered. When Daddy had been alive. Before he'd become ill. Long before. So they could become legends, so *Daddy* could.

So tall, so handsome, so strong and good and funny and true. Like all the heroes in the storybooks. Mom had told her stories, her legends, over and over again, to her and to Peggy. That was what life was all about. That was the only life that meant anything.

And I bought it. Gulped it right down, every last bit of it. It had to be that way. Hadn't Mommy said so? Hadn't Daddy been exactly what she'd said?

For Peggy it had been different. For Peggy it had been too much; too unattainable. So unattainable that she naturally went in the opposite direction; sought men who could never be what the legendary Daddy had been, what the legendary husband should be. *Just the opposite of me.*

Terrence. What a straw man she'd created. They'd known each other for so short a time, and even during the little time they'd had together, how much had they learned about each other? All those long silences, arms about each other as they walked, or fingers intertwining as they gazed silently at each other across a small table in a luncheonette, she with a cup of coffee, he with milk or a soda. True, she'd met no one like him then, and no one since. And hadn't Peggy felt the same way? *No. She'd been a kid. Just a twerp, a starry-eyed preadolescent. How could she have had any judgment?*

Frances stopped herself. *No. Even then, Peggy was remarkable at reading people. You used to tell her she was almost like a witch. Three seconds with them and she had them taped. Remember? The times you laughed at her and told her she was wrong, had really missed by a mile this time out? And then found she hadn't?*

Just a few moments and she knew them. Seemed to know all about them. *Except the men in Peggy's own life.* There she'd guess wrong so consistently they'd often laughed about it, Peggy shaking her head ruefully as she giggled.

Still. To have told Jeff all about it, and then let yourself drive past where he lives. It's a sickness, that's all. Thanks, Mom. That's right; blame it on Mom.

Frances rose, her mouth set firmly. It was all over.

She'd *make* it all over. As she entered the living room the phone rang.

She picked it up. "Hello?"

"Frances."

It was his voice. She felt her lips begin to tremble.

"Frances, this is Terrence. Look, I've tried not to do this. Tried to work it out by myself. Talked to other people, friends here at work. But it hasn't done any good. I can't stop thinking about you, Frances."

She said nothing, just stood there, the receiver to her ear, listening, waiting for his next words. It was as if she were back in those years, his voice no different now than it had been then; deep, warm, *caring.*

"I've taken the day off. On the chance I could see you. Just to talk it out. That's all. Just to talk it out, get rid of it that way."

Like me, she thought.

"That's all," he continued. "Nothing would happen. I promise you. Bring your little boy. Bring David."

She closed her eyes and breathed deeply. Then she told him a place. It was a scenic turnoff, just ten miles distant. He said he knew it.

They each agreed to leave immediately. He had moved, he told her, casually giving her his new address, and his new apartment was a little nearer to their meeting place than her home was. He'd be waiting, he told her, assured her.

David had always leapt at the chance to go someplace in the car, anyplace. But as they left the house, he began to whine and complain. "No go," he protested, "No go."

He cried almost the whole way there. Frances' nerves were rubbed raw by the sound, guilt providing an additional scraping of the wounds, lacerating them. *I shouldn't be doing this.* She knew she shouldn't . . . but she was. Talking it out would do no good. Not for her. Not now. Not anymore. Even as she'd agreed to the meeting, she'd been sure of it. And still she was going.

She neared the turnoff, slowed, and pulled onto the hilly, curving road that led to it. In seconds she was at the top. Reaching it, she saw, as she'd expected, and hoped, his was the only car there. He was standing alongside it, everything about him *expectant.* Cautiously, on the unlikely chance someone she knew would turn up, she parked a hundred feet away from him.

David's cries turned to yowls when she tried taking him out of his car seat. Angrily she pushed him back into it, crying "All right, stay there!" *He'll be just as safe there as with me,* she tried to persuade herself. But then he began to scream in real terror, and this time when she reached for him, he grabbed at her frantically.

By the time she had him out, Terrence had reached the car. David saw him, his eyes opened wide, he cried out once, and then hid his face, buried it deeply in her shoulder. She didn't know how much more she could take, and it must have shown in her expression.

Terrence's eyes were serious, his voice compassionate. "Maybe this isn't the time. I don't even know why I bothered you . . . selfish," he said, murmuring the last word, more to himself than to her.

She shook her head. "It's all right." There was a picnic bench nearby. She motioned toward it, and he nodded.

The weathered wood and concrete bench was near the edge of the overlook. Beyond it, the rolling New Jersey hills folded away, mile after mile, rectangular patches of shining green alternating with the darker, more muted greens of the forests. Scattered houses added flashes of white and red. Above it all rode an intensely blue sky. She lingered a bit, waiting till she saw which side of the table Terrence approached, then deliberately seated herself across from him.

Frances tried to put David down on the seat beside her, but, almost desperately, he pushed his way back onto her lap and again buried his face against her, still refusing to look at Terrence. He'd always been such a very friendly boy, almost too friendly, smiling and waving at each new face he saw, ready to engage everyone he met in conversation. Now he was silent, his forehead pressing so hard against her clavicle that it pained her. She tried to ignore all of it, attempted to keep her temper, restrain herself, be motherly.

This time Terrence seemed older. There were lines on his forehead and about his eyes that she hadn't noticed before. Despite herself, her gaze fixed on them for several moments, played along them, slowly, tenderly. "Do you remember our first date?" he began. "On the way home, I mean? We took a bus, and then got off at the nearest stop and began walking toward your house?"

She nodded, remembering it clearly, achingly, knowing what he was going to say next, certain of it.

"I had my arm around you. You were talking—I don't remember about what. And I suddenly found myself whirling you into my arms, hugging you—hugging you so wildly. It—It just happened. Spontaneously, without any thought. I was so filled with the wonder of you, so charged with exuberance."

"I remember," she told him, her voice small.

A breeze rustled past her, and somehow it seemed to be the same breeze she'd felt a little later that night long ago, as they stood at her doorway, staring into each other's eyes.

"When I kissed you at the door," he said, his eyes fully upon her, as soft and as searching as they had been on that night, "I was far from spontaneous. I remember being so careful about where I put my hands: one around your waist, the other on your back. Made sure I found your lips before I closed my eyes. You were the first girl I'd ever kissed."

She'd known she'd been the first. He'd never told her, no one had. But she'd known. Had simply *known*. She had kissed boys before. But no kiss had ever been like that. She thought of Jeff. She loved Jeff—*I do love Jeff*, she reminded herself—but with him it had been different. Their kisses had been hungry, physical. With Terrence it had been wholly different. It had been spiritual, almost devoid of any physicality but tenderness. And in no other way she'd known, it had been *equal*—the two of them the same, neither one dominant, neither one soft and yielding.

"We never did more than kiss," he went on, obviously uncomfortable, but just as obviously needing to say it, to get it all out. "But I wanted so much to go to bed with you. From that first night, I yearned for it." He shook his head slowly. "But not for the sex. Not so much for that, anyway, although of course that was there, too. But what I really wanted, really yearned for, was the lying with after."

Instantly her eyes moistened, and she glanced away.

Bob and Chris. Two names out of—how many? What had been the odds on the two of them coming up with exactly the same names? Yet one day he had told her, "Our names don't seem right. Not for each other. They should be Bob and Chris." And days before she had had the same thought, had kept it to herself. That their names weren't right. That they should be . . . *Bob and Chris.* And now this.

"For the lying with after." She'd never expressed that thought, those words to him, either; had never had the chance, their romance cut off so soon. But "for the lying with after" . . . those had been her words, too. The exact words. The thing she'd yearned for. Then. Ever since.

"You're not making this any easier," she told him. But there was no demurral in her voice, no protest; only a statement of fact.

"I wish I could. I'm trying," he told her, and then, "I *think* I'm trying. I *tell* myself I'm trying. A *part* of me is, anyway." He looked away, his eyes tracing the curving, distant hills, and then seeming to linger just beyond them . . . linger in another place, another world.

"I barely knew you," he resumed, and once again it was as if their minds had become one, her thoughts his thoughts, his thoughts hers . . . "We hardly spoke—I was too smitten, I guess," he added with a half smile, a smile at once apologetic and heart-quickening. "I never really knew much about you. Met your mother, your sister, but that was almost all of it. I keep telling myself that you're just someone I've made up, a fantasy I've created. That the person I've thought about, dreamed about all these years, the person

I've—" He hesitated, and she knew he'd been going to say "loved."

". . . that that person isn't the real you. But then," he concluded helplessly, "I see you, and none of that seems true."

David had begun to squirm in her arms, and bang his head against her. Now a series of whines and cries issued from him. "Hush, darling," she crooned, but that only seemed to infuriate him. He shook his head back and forth, went into a paroxysm of rage and tears. She looked helplessly at Terrence. "I'm sorry."

She stood and lowered David to the ground, hoping he'd stop, that his normal intense curiosity would take over as he found himself among the unfamiliar grass and rocks. But instead he threw himself down on the ground and went into a tantrum, something he'd never done before.

Frances knelt beside him, ran her hand over his body, his forehead, trying to soothe him, but it didn't help. Then she picked him up, and he began to subside. Until, looking up, he saw Terrence, and again began to squirm, to shake his head and yowl. Frustration, embarrassment, anger flashed through Frances. It was all she could do to keep herself from shaking David violently, scream at him to stop. Distraught, she turned to Terrence. "I'm sorry," she said. "I don't know what's wrong. He's never like this."

Terrence's nod was sympathetic, understanding.

"I'd better go," she told him. "I don't know why I—I don't know . . ." She found she was unable to say anything more; instead whirled and walked quickly back to the car.

He accompanied her. After she'd strapped David in, she turned and, as David screamed, found herself standing only inches from Terrence. He bent forward and kissed her lightly on the lips, his hands gently gripping her shoulders. He remained there, not moving, as she drove away.

Chapter
15

Frances had been back in the house for only a few moments when Jeff arrived. He was hours early.

"That damn Texas thing is still a mess," he told her. "They want me to go there for a few days—maybe longer. Don't know exactly when I'll be back." As he stared at her, his face seemed to darken. "Maybe it would be a good idea if you didn't stay alone," he said slowly. "You know, with the things that have gone on."

Her mind became paralyzed, muddled, refused to think clearly. Somehow she thought he was referring to her and Terrence.

He saw the blankness in her eyes. "I mean about the kitten. And what happened here while we were away. Of course it's not likely they had anything to do with each other, that anything could happen . . . but still . . . Maybe you could stay with Peggy. Or have her bunk out here."

She hadn't told him about the rift. Now she found herself wondering if he knew, had known all along. If Peggy had told him and he was playing the innocent. Suggesting the two sisters spend these nights together, knowing she'd have to refuse. Was he really going to Texas? Or was he going to Peggy's? "I'll be all right," was all she told him.

David was himself again and he stood and watched as his father packed. "Daddy's suitcase," he said several times, but Jeff, intent on what he was doing, didn't seem to hear him.

Frances didn't try to help. By now Jeff had it down to a science, was probably better than she was at arranging his clothes so that they'd be wrinkle-free when removed from the luggage. He left the room for a moment and came back with his toilet articles. He began stuffing them into the small bag he had for that purpose. "Cologne, too?" she asked, trying to keep her voice calm, unfreighted. He almost never wore it at home.

"Just in case my deodorant wears off. It gets pretty hot down there." He grinned nonchalantly.

When he left, he held her very tightly, kissed her very hard. *Too* tightly? *Too* hard? She stared into his eyes, trying to read them. Something happened as she did it; something crept into them; an oddness, as if something had just twisted inside him. *Or is he simply reacting to the way I'm looking at him?*

David clutched Jeff's leg all through the good-bye, then begged, "Daddy take me, too, Daddy take me, too," over and over again. It was another thing he'd never done before.

When Jeff left, it was too soon to begin making dinner, and she couldn't think of anything else to busy herself with. What she longed to do was to go into her bedroom, shut the door, fall onto the bed and try to sort out everything that was racing through her mind, torturing her.

She lay down on the living room couch, but almost instantly David was at her, talking to her, asking questions, crawling all over her, demanding her full attention. He wasn't really acting any differently than usual, but somehow it didn't *feel* the same. There was an intensity about him, as if he were deliberately forcing himself on her.

And yet . . . *was* he doing anything differently? Or was it all in her head? Was what she'd seen in Jeff all fantasy, too, conjured up by the guilt she was feeling because of Terrence?

It came to her all at once, with terrible clarity. *No. There* is *no* guilt. She sat there, stunned, sure. *I feel no guilt at all.* Granted, there was turmoil, indecision, agony. But no guilt. She felt no guilt about anything that had happened between the two of them. None of the reality that had happened, none of the feelings, the fantasies. There was nothing wrong about any of it. It was all clean, pure.

And that purity is tearing your marriage apart. Maybe even your motherhood. But despite that thought, her fingertips went to her lips, as they had several times on the drive home from the overlook. The magic there was gone now, of course. If Jeff hadn't come home so early, kissed her when he arrived, and again when he left, so hard . . . Almost as if he'd known, was deliberately trying to erase the lingering presence of Terrence's lips upon hers. *As if he'd known,* she told herself again.

"Getting a little bugs, aren't you?" she found herself muttering savagely under her breath as David played near her feet. There was no way Jeff could have known about their kiss. No way. And yet . . .

Finally it *was* time for dinner, and she gratefully lost

herself in its preparation. While serving it, she found herself expecting David to pick at his food, found herself already halfway on the defensive. But instead he tore at it voraciously, ate far more than he usually did. She even wound up having to give him some of her potatoes.

She took her time washing up, and then gave David his bath, lingering with that, too. He had become his normal calm, happy self, and while she bathed him he sang, chattered, and played with great concentration with one of his plastic boats. After she'd dressed him in his pajamas, she asked him, without expecting to, "Would you like to go to Aunt Peggy's?"

The first traces of sleepiness had already appeared on his small face, but at those words his eyes brightened and he nodded happily. Watching him, Frances found herself wondering if she'd have preferred that he told her no.

As she drove toward her sister's, Frances did all she could to keep from asking herself just why she was doing this. If she was going there to effect a reconciliation, the normal, wiser thing to do would have been to call first. And if she were driving there to see if Jeff's car was in the driveway . . .

She didn't allow herself to dwell on this last, about whether she *wanted* to find it there, so she could be freed, could run, no longer bound by anything, to Terrence . . .

The slow descent from dusk to night was just beginning, and Frances found herself detouring, turning onto lonely country roads she wasn't familiar with, waiting. Waiting for dark. She'd be less visible then. Less visible for . . . whatever she had in mind. She still had no idea of what it was, didn't want to know.

She glanced back into the rearview mirror, adjusted it so she could see David. But by now it was too dark to make him out. From all appearances, he was asleep. She saw a road ahead that she guessed would eventually bring her into Peggy's neighborhood, and turned right onto it. For the first time there were other cars on the road, and in the glare of approaching headlights, she glanced up again into the mirror. David's eyes were open.

Another quarter mile went by, and suddenly she knew where she was. She made another right, then a left and a right. She was on Peggy's road. She slowed, took her time passing the scattered houses that preceded Peggy's, driving as near to the right, as much in the shadows, as she could. She realized she still wasn't sure why she had come.

She reached the house. There was no sign of Jeff's car. Nor of Peggy's. There were no lights in the house, nor were the outside lights on.

Frances kept going, drove to the end of the road and made a U-turn at the dead-end, rather than going left as she could have done. She retraced her route, patiently, measuredly, as if somehow in those brief moments since she'd passed the house, something might have changed. But of course nothing had.

She would go home and put David to bed. Then she would turn on the television set and watch whatever she could find on the screen. Turn off her mind until she knew she could no longer stay awake. And in the morning she'd be all right. *Might* be.

That was when she began to hear David. He was singing. His voice was quiet, and she could barely make out the words. And yet . . . they almost seemed

. . . *Was* he singing it, over and over again? "Mommy talked to the man . . . Mommy kissed the man . . ."

As they passed a streetlight she looked into the rear-view mirror. David's eyes were wide open. He was still singing. Chanting.

Chapter
16

THE NEXT MORNING AFTER BREAKFAST, FRANCES TOOK David for a walk, determined to get outside, while it was still relatively cool, into the clean, fresh country air. On their way they ran into Mrs. Emenesky. She'd come to put out a letter, was raising the red flag on her mailbox to alert the postman. She smiled as she saw them, well-worn creases deepening around her eyes. "Good morning," she sang out in a cheerful, neighborly way.

"Good morning. Beautiful day, isn't it?" Frances cried back, hopeful.

"Oh, yes. Beautiful. And your child is beautiful, too. Hello, David," she said, simultaneously waving to him and turning to climb the long dirt driveway to her house.

Frances tried to think of something that would stop her, a statement or question which would initiate an exchange of words, an exchange that in turn would develop into a conversation. And perhaps even an invitation. To Mrs. Emenesky's house, to her own, it made no difference. So long as she could be with someone else, talk with them. About inconsequential things, *normal* things.

But nothing would come. Frances stood there, watching the old woman make her way up the gullied drive, her back bent double with the effort.

"That lady loves me," David announced emphatically.

"Yes, she does," Frances told him. *If only some of that feeling carried over to me.*

There were things to do at home, plenty of things. Beds to be made, clothes to be washed, rooms to be dusted, wastebaskets to be emptied. Instead, shortly after they got back from their walk, she put David into his car seat. They'd spend the day at the mall. *Let me try that. Get away for a while. From all this solitude. From all this time to think.* Away from the house. Away from the loneliness.

They drove to the Winslow mall, thirty miles away. It was a long trip for David, but he held up well, staring intently out at the scenery almost all of the time, eagerly crying out about animals and small children as they passed them.

The mall was huge and colorful, all of it enclosed, marvelously air-conditioned; the temperature outside had reached ninety-four. David attracted his usual admiring stares and wonder-filled compliments. He was her marvelous little boy again, his eyes bright, shining with curiosity and intelligence. Twice he stopped to speak to boys no bigger than himself; his voice music while he spoke to them as he would longtime friends. Each time the boys, David's age but nowhere near his brightness, edged to their mothers and stared, mouths open, saying nothing. It was during the second encounter that Frances realized, for the first time, a small tide of guilt welling within her, that her son was reaching the age where he'd need friends, friends of his age. And where she lived, there was no one, no one at all, for him.

Sitting in a small fast food restaurant inside the mall, she regarded him with tender sadness as he ate his tiny hamburger and sipped at the malted she'd bought him. It had been the first real thought, the first realization, of his growing up; soon he'd no longer be completely hers, content with just his mommy during the day.

Thinking about all this, she was still subdued as they drove home. *But at least,* she told herself, *these are normal thoughts, normal feelings.* And that was good. The excursion seemed to have worked.

She took no chances when they got home, however; busied herself as soon as they arrived. Near dinnertime, Jeff called. He sounded cheerful, vigorous, optimistic about all the problems, almost too loving. But she found she was able to react rationally about the last. *Well, why not? Maybe he's a little uncertain, after what you told him about Terrence. Maybe he's trying to make up to you for whatever he's afraid he hadn't been giving you. Lighten up. That's all it is. He's not faking it, not trying to fool you, lull you.*

"No, I still don't know how long I'll be stuck here. Could end any minute, or go on forever. Already feels like it has. Wish me luck. *Us* luck," he told her just before he hung up.

After dinner she called Peggy twice, but there was no answer. She decided to go through the same routine she had the night before. Once David was safely tucked away, she got into bed and turned on the TV, deliberately choosing a channel that was running sitcoms that night. She didn't feel capable of handling anything stronger.

She fell asleep before her last show was over, the television still on. The sleep was fitful; full of jagged half dreams, dreams that tantalized her, called to her. But as she approached them, they would fragment, dissolve. And then a new one would appear, off-kilter, disturbing, just beyond her reach. Voices she couldn't quite recognize, faces she almost did . . . Finally, fretfully, she forced herself awake.

The TV was still on. It seemed to be a continuation of her dream. Groggily, she realized it was the eleven o'clock news; a woman on the screen was talking about a murder. The name of the town sounded familiar. She'd never been too good on geography, on the names and locations of places . . . but it sounded like something nearby. And then she understood. They were talking about a fourth murder. Another woman, again stripped bare, again with a circle of gold about her battered throat.

The remote control was inches away. She reached for it, clicked the TV off. She had to think. Because something had sprung into her mind, making her bolt upright in the bed, adrenaline exploding out all the last vestiges of sleep.

Jeff wasn't home tonight. He hadn't been home last night.

That's crazy. Why are you thinking like this? But telling herself that did no good. She tried to think of the other times. Had he been away then, too? She thought so, but when she tried to pin down the dates, they all seemed to run together. The memory of that magazine in his drawer intruded itself, and she heard herself moan.

His calendar. She rose and walked over to it. This time she didn't stop herself. Each time she found she could fix a date in her mind, she looked it up. The first two times, as she stared at the page, she felt more of a numbness steal through her. The third time didn't equate, but immediately she remembered the third body had been found days after the death. *Bucks County*. His disappearance that night . . . Perhaps coming all the way back here. Perhaps . . . for no reason she could think of, except as some kind of maniacal explosion . . . perhaps *Jeff* had torn the house apart. And then she remembered.

The suitcases.

He hadn't put them in the trunk, had insisted it was easier just to stash them in the backseat. Had that been the real reason? The true reason he hadn't wanted to open the trunk?

Her suspicions about Martin's disappearance came back to her. No connection, of course, she told herself, to the women. And then . . . *Unless it had . . . begun something, loosened something in Jeff.* She pushed the pages of the calendar back, went deeper into it. There was the date. The date Martin had disappeared. "New Mexico," it read.

It came back to her now. He *had* been away. Or had told her he was. She'd had to tell him about Martin when he returned. Had told him about it when it still didn't seem like much; more gossip than dire news, assuming Martin had gone off with a woman, would be back in a day or two. Or at least that's what Jeff had suggested. She tried to reach back, to remember his words, recapture his expression when she'd told him, but nothing came.

She let her fingers trail out of the calendar, the

pages falling back in place. She continued staring at it. *None of it means anything, of course. It's all coincidence. Life is full of coincidence.* Jeff was a normal man. As normal as anyone she'd ever known. Maybe more than that; she'd never known anyone to react more calmly in times of stress, even of danger. *Or is that just a part of a dead coldness deep inside him, a coldness I was never able to see?* She'd read about psychopaths; their deadly charm, their total lack of conscience, of humanity.

The noise downstairs, when it came, could have been a rafter shifting position; a muffled, cracking noise. On another night she could have borne it; felt a brief, temporary fear, maybe even a longer carryover of uneasiness, but she could have borne it. When it came again, she reached for the phone.

She dialed Peggy's number, let it ring seven, eight, nine times. No answer. She tried again, on the chance she'd misdialed. Then she dialed again, quickly, not bothering to see if there was another noise. If she heard one, she wasn't sure she could survive it. The number she dialed was the operator's. They handled information at this time of night. When the operator came on, Frances asked if she had a new listing. For Horgan, she said. Terrence Horgan.

She waited till she saw his headlights approach, heard his car turn into the driveway. Then she jerked open the bedroom door, flew down the stairs. It wasn't till she was at the front door, fumbling with the lock, that she realized she was wearing nothing but a nightgown. *Too late now.* She opened the door to him. "Thank you. Oh, thank you for coming!" She began to sob.

Terrence's arms opened and she fell into them. Almost immediately the sound of a car somewhere off in the distance reached her. It was coming up the road, would pass the house. Quickly she released herself and drew him inside with her, where he couldn't be seen.

She shut the door, locked it, then turned away from it and faced him. He was standing in the middle of the living room, his expression concerned, wondering, patient. He said nothing, waited for her to speak. She had given no indication over the phone as to why she needed him here, had simply begged him to come.

Shaking her head, she told him tremulously, "I can't tell you why I wanted you here. Please don't ask me. All I can tell you is that I'm terribly, terribly afraid." She tried to laugh, but the result was grotesque; high-pitched, strangled. "There's probably nothing to it at all. Absolutely nothing. In fact if I told you about it, all about it, you'd probably back away from me and start looking for the nearest exit."

"Not a chance," he told her. "No chance of that at all."

A shiver ran down her spine as the words came at her, and she knew the feeling had nothing to do with fear. Not the kind of fear she'd been feeling, anyway. It was a fear of herself now. *What've I done? What ever possessed me to call him? To bring him here?* It must have been pure hysteria. She'd tell him to go, that she was all right now, apologize for being such a ninny.

Instead she said, "Would you like some coffee?"

He declined, and she suggested he seat himself in the living room. He sat at one end of the couch. Watching, she told herself she should sit away from him, on one of the chairs. Instead, she took her seat at the sofa's opposite end.

As she looked at Terrence, she thought about Jeff. He'd given her no definite time when he might be back. For all she knew, he could be headed here now. And if he found her here with Terrence? On the same couch, only inches apart? In her nightgown?

Jeff had never been violent with her. But she'd seen him when his temper had been aroused. Saw again his face flushing, his neck thickening, his muscles bulging, eyes dangerous, barely able to contain himself. Again she shivered, but still she remained seated where she was.

She began to speak. "I shouldn't put you through this," she told him. "If my husband—if Jeff comes home . . ."

"It's all right," he assured her. And somehow it did give her assurance.

Her next words, she knew before she said them, would be like stepping off a foothold without looking down, without watching to see if the next step was just a few inches below, a drop of a few feet, or a plummet that would fall away into forever. "I'm afraid I haven't been the same . . . haven't been, you know, calm, *every day* . . . haven't been who I had become for so long . . . since I saw you again that first time."

"I'm sorry," he said. But then he smiled, a small sad smile that had no expectation in it. "But not completely. I can't help being a little glad that it's happened to you, too."

Her eyes were wholly on him now. "I have a good marriage, Terrence," she told him, wondering as she said it whether it was to inform him or to convince herself. "I know I'm lucky with it. *In* it. Whatever its imperfections, and there really aren't many. I wouldn't want to do anything to jeopardize it. That's why I haven't. Why I'm not doing it now. Why I don't plan to." She saw herself telling him this, saw herself saying it while she sat there with him, barely inches apart, her bare feet tucked up under her flimsy nightgown, nothing beneath that thin scrap of cloth. Was she already hurtling downward, blinding herself to what she was really in the process of doing? She didn't know, had no idea, but she realized then that her lips had parted, that breathing was becoming more difficult for her.

Did I truly hear noises before? She'd heard nothing since she'd called, nor since he'd arrived. *Did I make it all up, so that I could use it as an excuse to bring him here? Tonight? While I'm here alone?*

But . . . if I didn't know I was doing it . . . then it's not my fault. Not what's happened so far. Maybe not even whatever's to come. She stared helplessly at a painting on the opposite wall; a farmhouse, serene, untroubled. *You're lying to yourself, of course,* she told herself, and then found she didn't care much. It was as if, in some odd way, it was already out of her hands. She would just watch, and wait, and let whatever happened happen. None of it was under her control anymore. She was a ship adrift, wholly at the mercy of the sun and the wind and the tides. Why worry about a tomorrow that might never come? A feeling of freedom, a freedom such as she'd never known, began to wash over her.

She gazed at him, and he at her, neither of them speaking. There seemed to be no movement, no effort on her part, no shifting of her body, and yet as the moments wore on, she found herself somehow closer and closer to him, and finally, with a movement that felt like a sigh, she rested herself against him, felt his arm encircle her. They still said nothing. There was no need for speech. Just as it was, it was all there, a complete world. Nothing more was needed, nothing more was necessary. A feeling of total peace came over her. She was home. *For now*, she was home.

Her body relaxed against his, softened, and she nestled her head beneath his, heard the faint sound of his breathing, smelled the sweetness of his breath. Her eyes began to close, and again she felt as if she were adrift on a great ocean, but wholly shorn of aloneness, of risk. She would be safe now, she knew. Completely, wholly safe. She sighed, lowered a hand onto his thigh and drifted peacefully into sleep.

Chapter
17

"Mommy!"

David's first call woke her. Frances' eyes opened, and for a moment, not sure of where she was, she was aware only of a serenity that seemed wholly new to her. Then her eyes saw his arm, still enfolding her.

Frances glanced up. His eyes met hers. She had the impression he'd just awakened, too, his gaze instantly clear and alert. As his eyes found hers, a soft smile curled the corner of his lips. "That's David," she told him, her voice hushed, as if to prevent the shattering of a spell. "I have to go to him. And I'm sorry . . . but I think it'd be best if you go now."

He looked at her searchingly.

"I'm all right. I'm all right now," she told him.

He nodded, gently kissed the top of her head, and rose. There was a great, resigned sadness on his face. "I know this is the last time I'll ever see you," he told her. "But I'm very grateful for your calling me; for these few hours."

Frances nodded hurriedly, wanting to go to David; wanting Terrence to leave. *Now, immediately*. It was already becoming light. People would be going to work, driving past the house, seeing his car there.

She waved toward the door, indicating that he leave, as she moved quickly toward the stairs. Reaching them, she turned. He was already nearly out the door. "Good-bye. And thank you," she told him.

He nodded, and then he was gone.

Upstairs, hurrying toward David's room, she heard Terrence's car start up. Rushing in, she ignored David and went to the farthest window. She was just in time to see him drive away. As his car disappeared, Frances found herself fussing with the curtain, as if somehow it was important that she make David think that was why she'd run to the window. Then she turned to him. She was with her little boy now. She and David, in their lovely house together. And soon David's Daddy would be home. Her husband. Jeff and David with her. And they'd all be together, the three of them, be all right from here on, *safe*. Because she'd exorcised all the craziness last night, still felt the serenity of her time with Terrence.

Then during breakfast—David was excitedly telling her about a monkey that went bang!—she had no idea what he meant—an image flashed through her mind. A vivid, ghastly picture of Jeff driving in a car, something going wrong, and his crashing into a light pole, dying. Then a second scene, of his body on the ground, lying where it had been flung by the crash, his head bloodied, people standing around helplessly, knowing they were too late.

Through all of it David prattled on, his face glowing in the early morning sunlight, telling her now about a dog that went "ruff, ruff," smiling at his mother as if she were a kind woman, a good woman, a perfect mother . . . a perfect wife.

My God. I want that to happen. That's why I'm thinking it. So I can be free. Free of any fear of losing my son. Free to spend the rest of my life with Terrence.

She quickly left the table and pretended to busy herself with the dishes. She shook her head wryly, bitterly. *What's wrong with me? How can I possibly think of attracting, of keeping, a man like Terrence? Because he's a good man, a compassionate man. Sure, he thinks he loves me. But in time he'd know, find out . . . what I am, what I can become . . .*

But the thoughts wouldn't go away. During the rest of the morning and early afternoon, awful, terrible pictures kept stabbing into her mind; Jeff suddenly becoming ill, succumbing . . . his plane crashing . . . no survivors . . . *My God, I'd kill a whole planeload of people just to get what I want . . . What I think I want. What I fantasize I want. There's no reality to what you're thinking, no reality at all . . .* But then she would see Terrence's eyes, and hear his words again, feel the security of his arm about her as she slept, and she knew there was a reality. He did love her. Thought he did. Loved who he thought she was. As she did him. *Only with Terrence, there's no doubt. I know what he was then. And he's the same now.*

She tried Peggy at home, and then at the office. She had to talk to someone. There was no one else. No way she could tell any of *this* to Jeff . . . not this time. It had gone too far. Too far for that . . .

"Huntington School."

"Peggy Tighe please."

"I'm sorry. She's on leave. Can anyone else help you?"

Frances knew when Jeff's secretary went out for lunch. Very deliberately she waited till that time and then called his office. "Jeff Sommers please."

"Just a moment please."

A treacle of music spilled tinnily into her ear, catching at her nerve endings, twisting them.

"Mr. Sommers' office." Frances found she'd timed it right. The voice was unfamiliar to her.

She was able to use her own voice, not clumsily try to change it. "May I speak to him, please?"

"I'm sorry. He's out of town."

"Do you have a number where he can be reached?"

The music resumed, and she gritted her teeth. David was calling to her from the playroom. "Just a minute," she yelled back, hurling the words as quickly as she could, stupidly afraid the operator would catch her in the act, instantly understand that she was a suspicious wife, a darkly hopeful wife . . .

The woman came back on and gave her a number. Frances nodded, and hung up. It was the one Jeff had given to her before he'd left. So there must be another explanation for Peggy's absence, she thought. Unless the two of them were so besotted with each other that Jeff had taken her to Texas with him. But that wasn't likely. She knew from the past what long, hard hours he'd worked on those trips.

Not only Jeff had told her, she reminded herself. Charlie Bergman, too. Or had Charlie been covering up for Jeff? One man backing up another's story, hanging together the way men did. *Maybe Jeff has been cheating on me all along, one woman after another. Or just . . . Peggy.*

Her head began to throb, so intense that it blurred her vision. She stumbled her way into the playroom, scooped David up and went with him up to the bathroom, where she found herself some aspirin. He watched the procedure with fascination. He knew what she used the small white pills for, and after a moment, as he sat on her lap, he reached up and patted her forehead tenderly.

She pulled away from him as the tears sprang out, quickly set him down on the floor and buried her face in a nearby towel, rubbed her eyes hard as he said, uncertainly, "Mommy wet?"

Frances drew her face away from the towel, hoping she'd look all right to him. "Mommy loves you," she answered.

She felt herself beginning to calm down, to think more clearly. Holding him in her arms and crooning to him, she carried David back downstairs and into the kitchen, where she began to make sandwiches. After she'd filled a thermos and wrapped some cookies in Saran, she announced to him, "David and Mommy are going to go on a picnic." He smiled up at her expectantly, a little doubtfully. It took her a moment to realize that the word must be new to him.

She explained what picnics were as they drove to the state forest. Trying to make it sound like fun, she told him they could sit on the grass and eat, wouldn't have to sit in chairs or at tables. "We can just eat on the grass."

"Like kittycats." David nodded, with some excitement, and she agreed it would be just like kittycats.

It was midsummer now, and the park was more crowded than she'd ever seen it, though it was so huge there was still more than enough room for everyone.

Children ran gaily over the grass, crying out to each other and to their parents. Teenagers spun Frisbees or stood and kissed for long, long moments. College students and other young people in their twenties were there, too, embracing, strolling, playing games.

There were fathers and husbands on vacation; young men with their wives, a number of the women in their light summer clothing visibly pregnant. Children hung on their fathers, talking to them, imploring them, as the husbands gazed at their wives, smiled, cast suggestive glances.

As Frances watched, she found envy creeping into her. How easy it all seemed, how lucky they were. Did they realize how lucky? Husband, wife, children. Units. Individual units of one that combined into whole units of one. Together, nothing dividing them, untroubled by any confusion of thought, ugliness of spirit, sickness of mind . . .

They picnicked first, David enchanted with the whole idea of it. He became very serious and chatty, conducting a long conversation that consisted mainly of exclamations and pointings—at the boys and girls his age, at the dogs that raced about the large, open meadow, at the Frisbees soaring gracefully through the blue, blue air.

After lunch she took him to the small amusement park and tried as hard as she could to concentrate on him, to watch his small, delighted face as they rode the miniature roller coaster, the not much larger merry-go-round, she standing alongside him, hands protectively near him, but allowing him the sensation of sitting astride a horse all on his own. His face was suffused with pleasure.

Slowly, it began to happen. She felt more and more

that she was back to where she'd once been; where she'd been on that long-ago morning just before she'd seen Terrence for the first time. As they left the park, the idea of Jeff having anything to do with those women's deaths seemed absurd; three o'clock in the morning imaginings. Headed toward the station wagon, she stopped and hugged David for several long, long moments. He didn't object.

As she drew near the house, she saw the Toyota parked at the far end of the driveway. Jeff was home. For an instant there was the memory of the car that had been there only hours before; Terrence's car. But then she was all right again, and by the time she was halfway up the porch stairs, Frances was eager and expectant, ready to begin all over again.

When she entered, Jeff was standing in the middle of the living room. David shouted to him, and she began to greet him. Then she saw his expression. She fell silent.

Jeff moved to them, took David out of her arms and began talking to him, ignoring her. As his son told him a clear-voiced, exclamatory tale of picnic and dogs and merry-go-round, Frances stood there without moving, watching. Jeff's gaze never left David's face, never strayed, even momentarily, to her.

Eventually Jeff carried David into the playroom. He remained there with him, his deep voice occasionally responding to something David said or pointed out. But the sound of his voice—from the moment he'd taken David in his arms—wasn't the sound she knew. There was something subdued about it, something lifeless.

For a long, long time Frances stood there, remained where she'd been from the time she'd entered. Finally she sank down onto the couch. The day's newspapers were spread out before her, one of the front page stories yet another one about the local murders. She glanced toward the headline, but none of the words seemed to mean anything. After a few moments her eyes left the newspaper and she stared unseeingly out the window.

She had no idea how long she sat there before Jeff returned. She watched him as he entered, her eyes unblinking, almost resigned, faintly echoing the dread that had risen inside her.

He stopped a few feet from her, still expressionless. "I saw one of our neighbors today," he told her. "He was driving down the road as I was coming home. Flagged me down."

Jeff waited a moment, watching her. Frances saw it now; his eyes were like his voice; wholly without life. She realized it was the first time he'd ever looked at her as he would have at someone who meant nothing to him; a stranger he was totally indifferent to.

"Told me he saw a man come into the house last night. Told me he saw the same guy drive away this morning."

You damned fool. You thought you were playing a game, an amusing little game that would hurt no one. Dreamed your stupid little dreams, prissed your way through life as if nothing was going on, smug in your fantasies, indulging yourself, as if you and what you got from life were all that mattered. And now you've lost your husband. And you're going to lose your home . . . there's no way you can afford to live here . . . And you may even lose your child.

But still, she tried to tell herself, as she looked up at Jeff, tears beginning to spill over from the corners of her eyes, *you've done nothing, absolutely nothing. You did nothing with Terrence to be ashamed of. Yes, you slept in his arms, but you might have done that with any friend, with your sister* . . .

She had come away from the park sure that all of this was over. Well, dammit, she'd *make* it over. She'd fight for what she now knew she wanted. For David, for her home. And . . . for Jeff. She swallowed once, twice, and then began to speak.

"I've been playing a dangerous game," she said softly. "But it's only been a game. That's all it was. And the game had very strict rules. Very strict. You know me, Jeff. You know I don't lie. It was a game, and I never broke those rules, not any of them, not once."

She told him all of it then. Left nothing out, not the brief kiss at the overlook, not her sleeping in Terrence's arms, not even the terrible, terrible daydreams of that morning, the unsought, unexplained visions of Jeff's death.

She told him, too, of the afternoon in the park. About what she'd realized, about how she'd finally understood how much it all meant to her. How all the rest had been a spoiled, self-indulgent caprice. Probably because she had been *too* happy, *too* content, *too* cared-for. Had needed something like this to make her realize just how much she had, how rich her life was. "Nothing happened, Jeff, nothing at all," she said, finally. "I love you. You're the one I love. You're the one I've always loved. You're my husband. I'm your wife."

Through all of it he stood there, not moving, his expression unchanged. When she was done, he nodded and said "All right." But he didn't go to her, and his voice was cold.

An hour later, as she was in the midst of housework,

Frances looked out the window and saw Jeff's car was gone. He'd asked her only one question during her long explanation. "Where does he live?"

His voice had been rough, his look dark, and she hadn't told him, had said it made no difference now, had pressed on with what she wanted to tell him, needed to. Now as she looked out the window, she remembered having told Jeff about Peggy's bumping into Terrence that time. She had told Peggy where Terrence was staying. It was possible Terrence had left his forwarding address at the motel.

As the thought came to her, she sprang to the phone. Quickly, frantically, she dialed Terrence's number. Jeff killing Terrence . . . Jeff going to prison . . . There was no answer. She tried Peggy. No answer there, either.

Her heart beginning to pound, she tried each of them again, and then again. After that she called the motel, asking if Mr. Horgan had left a forwarding address. The woman who answered said he hadn't, but her answer was guarded, unsatisfactory, and Frances begged her not to give any information to anyone who asked for it. As she hung up, David wandered into the room, announcing that he was hungry. Frances stared at him uncomprehendingly.

She'd drive to Terrence's. Stop Jeff before he did anything. And if he weren't there, wait till Terrence arrived. Warn him. "I'm hungry," David told her again, and this time she heard him. She held out her arms to him, as if that would be answer enough. She could hold him while she thought. But he pulled away petulantly. "I'm *hungry*," he told her again, this time his voice insistent.

Somehow she managed to make her way into the

kitchen, find him some cookies and milk, put him in his high chair. As she started to leave, not even quite sure what it was she was about to do, David called out. "Don't go away!" His tone was annoying, spoiled, bratty.

She felt a sudden urge to hit him as hard as she could with her open hand, knock him off his chair, into the glass patio door. She caught her hand as it was halfway up, stunned by her impulse.

After a moment, with great effort, she said, "We'll have another picnic. A snack picnic. In the living room." Frances lifted David out of his chair, carried him, the milk and the cookies into the living room.

Once there, she seated him on the rug, then arranged herself by him, the phone at her side. She'd try again. Just in case. She began to dial. David spilled his milk.

She started to weep. Everything in her wanted to drive directly to Terrence's, but she couldn't go there. She knew that. If Jeff saw her there, then it would very likely be all over; what chance that he'd believe her? Besides, she'd be forced to take David with her. If Jeff were armed, began firing . . . And, of course, the time that would be lost driving there, unable to call Terrence, warn him. She'd already racked her mind, trying to think of the name of Terrence's corporation, but nothing had come. She gazed dazedly at her little boy, who was shouting at her, over and over, "Mommy fix milk! Mommy fix milk!" He was near hysteria.

The paper towels were where they'd always been, but it took her several moments before she could locate them. Finally she blundered back into the living room, cleaned up the spill, somehow managed to fill another cup. She watched David with it this time, one hand ready as the other dialed Terrence. And then Peggy. And then Terrence again.

It was a nightmare that went on for hours. She had the radio on, to hear if she'd been too late—if something had already happened. Its noise, combined with David's petulance, made all of it the more nerveracking. He had never seemed more demanding. He was unwilling to let her out of his sight for a moment, constantly demanded her attention, threw his toys in fury at the telephone, which she kept dialing, over and over, afraid she might not reach anyone in time, afraid it might already be too late.

It lasted through dinner, Jeff still not back, Frances getting up every few moments to try the phone again. It lasted through David's bath; a hasty one so that she could get back to the phone. It lasted through the near hour it took for her to get him to sleep, trying to lull him, calm him, soothe him while every fiber in her was straining to get to the phone, to try again.

Finally David fell asleep, and she went to the phone in her room. As she reached out to dial, she looked down at her hand; blood was oozing out of the end of her index finger, the one she'd been using all day. Not bothering to bandage it, she promptly began dialing with her middle finger.

But nothing worked. It seemed useless now to try Peggy, but she did, trying again immediately after another fruitless attempt to reach Terrence.

She had both the radio and the TV on, the TV with the sound off, her eye on the screen in case anything were announced. Twice she pushed up the TV's sound to catch what she thought might be news; but each time it was about unrelated crimes.

A few minutes after midnight she was still at the

phone. She heard a car pull into the driveway. She hung up, sure that what she heard was the sound of Jeff's Toyota. Uncertain of what might happen, still clothed, she quickly threw herself onto the bed and waited. A minute later, when he entered the room, she faked sleep. She could hear him breathing heavily.

The lights went out almost immediately, Frances sensing the change through her closed lids. But there had been no sound of Jeff removing his clothes, and there was none now. Just the barest rustle of movement, and then silence.

For several minutes she lay there, waiting for him to come to bed, but he didn't. She was sure he was still in the room, thought she could hear the faint sound of his breathing. But she couldn't be certain; the radio was still on, masking most of whatever sounds there might be.

Finally, cautiously, she opened one of her lids a crack. The room was dark. Her eye roamed it, and came to a stop near the window. He was seated in the small chair near the sewing machine. He seemed to be facing toward her.

There was something looming and monstrous about his shadow, something chilling about his complete lack of movement and total quiet. Frances felt her heart begin to race, her breath quicken. She tried to stifle her breathing, afraid he would hear and realize she was awake, was bluffing, but it only seemed to make it worse.

Her lips began to form a word . . . and then stopped. She realized she was too afraid. Afraid of breaking into a future that might destroy her. If she broke into it *now*. Perhaps later . . . perhaps there would be more hope. In the morning. When he'd had time to think, become rational, calm . . . *In the meantime I'll lie here and watch him, be ready to run, to defend myself if I have to . . .*

But soon she found she was having trouble keeping the eye open. It would flutter, then close. She would force it open. A few moments later it would happen again. Over and over, each time a little sooner. *Must stay awake, must* . . . she thought. And then slept.

Chapter
18

FRANCES JERKED AWAKE. IT CAME TO HER, HER EYES STILL closed, that it had all been a dream. Some terrible, disconnected nightmare, a tortured shadow play involving Jeff, Terrence, and a golden chain. She had been tormented, terrified through it all, but hadn't known why. Finally, the fear had awakened her.

Her eyes blinked twice.

It was early morning. She saw Jeff. He was still sitting in the chair, still motionless. *That* hadn't been a dream. His eyes were open, and they were on her.

"Good morning, Frances," he told her. His voice was flat, without affect. "I've been sitting here all night," he told her, "watching you."

She lay there, still not moving, said nothing, waited . . .

"I didn't know what I was going to do," Jeff continued. "Didn't know what the next step was going to be." He shook his head slowly, as if to clear it. His eyes were sunken, shadowed, his lips dry, beginning to crack.

"I did the same thing when I drove away from

here," he told her. "Drove for hours . . . I don't even know where . . . trying to decide what to do. All that time . . . all the time I drove, all the time I sat here . . . All of that time spent thinking . . . and I didn't know what I was going to do. Till now. Till this minute . . . when I saw your eyes open, saw you wake up."

She continued to listen and to wait. Her feeling was no longer one of fear, but of a curious resignation. It was as if none of it mattered anymore. *Or is it*, she suddenly found herself wondering, *because I know Terrence is safe? Is that all that matters to me anymore?*

Jeff stirred, leaned toward her. "I looked at you and realized," he went on, ". . . I love you, Frances. I love you now and I always will. And David, too. He's part of it. A part of *us*. I don't want to know what happened between you . . . and . . . that guy. I don't want to know. I'm not going to think about it. Not anymore. Any of the things that I did that weren't right . . . things that might have caused all of this . . . any of the things I *didn't* do, those too, I want you to tell me all about them. All of them. I'll try to get them fixed, straighten this all out."

Frances opened her lips as if to speak, but he shook his head. "Not now. Not now, though. Too tired. And it's late. I have to get ready for work. Right now. It's still bad there."

He left the room, staggering a bit, as if with a great weariness. She had yet to speak a word to him.

Slowly Frances undressed and drew on a robe. She moved to the radio to turn it off. The news was on. She realized they were talking about a new murder. Another woman, so far unidentified. Also nude, also wearing a gold chain. *Accounts for the dream*, she thought without emotion, too drained from the anxiety of the day before, the restless night's sleep, the effects of Jeff's speech on her. *There must have been another report on it while I was asleep; affected my dream.*

David called out before she was halfway to the stairs. She went into his room, picked him up, put him on his little potty, and then carried him down to the kitchen. She avoided looking into his eyes. They were dark-ringed this morning, too, a reflection of his father's; as if David, too, had had little sleep, as if he, too, had realized, in some unconscious way, that he was a part of all this. She pressed him to her breast, held his small blond head against her, in agony remembering that horrible moment the day before; the blind rage that had suddenly filled her as he'd screamed for her to stay with him. That wouldn't happen again. *Couldn't. Ever.*

It wasn't till after Jeff had left that Frances fully realized she'd been unable to kiss him when he went, had turned her cheek as he'd sought her lips. He had said nothing, just nodded, the edge of his mouth twisted slightly.

After breakfast David seemed content to play by himself, and she found herself filled with a numbed gratitude. It would give her time to think, to figure out some way of pulling the pieces of her life back together. On the surface it was all right. *Should* be all right. She had Jeff now, and David. It could be the same again. Maybe not right away. It might take a little time, take *her* a little time. But eventually, soon, it could be the same, maybe even better . . . because maybe Jeff would be a little more gentle, a little more caring, and she a little more grateful . . .

And then, all at once, she moaned. The thought of the woman . . . the one on the radio . . . the one they'd found . . . the latest of them . . . That thought came to her. And another thought, a thought that came simultaneously, twinned, inseparable . . . *And Jeff was out of the house again.*

You're doing this deliberately. You want to wreck your marriage. This time as she listened to herself, she heard a certainty that hadn't been there before. *There's a sickness in you that wants to destroy the life you have with Jeff. Because he isn't perfect. Because in your sickness you think there's such a thing as a perfect man, a white knight, who can make everything right for you,* everything. *And of course there's no such thing.* But then, despite not wanting to, attempting to force the image away, she saw Terrence again, saw the clearness, the gentleness in his eyes, the caring . . .

She tried Peggy again, first at home, then at work. But the switchboard operator reported she was still away.

David's playroom was childproofed, but she rarely left him alone in there for very long. He was still too young. She went in and watched him as he played with his beloved cars and "men." *Your poor son. Because it's possible you're insane, you know. It's possible David has a mother who soon won't be able to take care of him, hold him, bring him up, teach him things . . .*

There was the sound of a car in the driveway. It wasn't Jeff's. Frances ran toward the front door and looked out.

Peggy.

Even as she opened the front door to greet her sister, relieved to see her, to know she was all right, she realized a part of her was feeling a crushing disappointment. That part of her that had hoped it would be Terrence.

Peggy's look as she got out of her car was hesitant, uncertain. Frances gave her a like smile.

That was all her sister needed. She rushed up to Frances and hugged her tightly. "Oh Jesus, Frannie, forgive me. I'm so sorry."

It was the first time Peggy had called her Frannie since they'd been kids. Frances felt the tears rush to her eyes, and let them fall, unashamedly. Peggy was crying, too, their tears commingling as they clutched each other.

"Aunt Peggy! Aunt Peggy!" David was at Peggy's feet now, looking up, his arms outstretched, his expression suddenly doubtful as he saw his beloved aunt's tears. But she jubilantly scooped him up into her arms and crushed him against her as he squealed in delight.

It was a diversion, and it helped. The two sisters' tears dried, even before they'd entered the house, where Peggy allowed David to show her his new cars and men.

"I never realized till that stupid night—*after* that night—how much you mean to me," Peggy told Frances as she simultaneously inspected and admired David's toys. She ran her fingers through his kittenlike hair. ". . . How much I love you. How much you've done for me. All my life—not just since the thing with Martin—well, Christ, I always knew, but I guess for a little while I forgot. Can you forgive me?" she finished, glancing up at her sister, anguished doubt and hope forming a silent entreaty.

"Forgive you? I did that the minute you drove up. Hell, long before that. Of course," Frances said, meaning it. Her whole world had flipped around again, was beginning to make sense all over again. David, Peggy, Jeff . . . if she hadn't turned him off as he left . . . "I've been trying to get you for days," she told Peggy.

"I've been away."

There was something in the way she said it, something in her voice, in her expression, that seemed odd. Frances stared at her.

"Had an affair. A blazer. Thought it was the real thing for a while."

"I'm sorry," Frances told her. Poor Peggy. So right about everything else in her life. So wrong about her men.

"But I was all wrong about it going in," Peggy continued, the odd tone of her voice, the look on her face, still there.

Jeff. She did *have an affair with Jeff. Oh Christ. Him sitting there all last night, watching me, trying to decide what the hell to do after he'd been screwing my own goddamn sister . . .*

"I'd always envied you for him. God, how wonderful I always thought he was. And he *was* wonderful. He was wonderful to me. Because that's what he is. But it didn't count. Because he loves you. Still does."

Sophisticated, Frances told herself. *I'm supposed to be sophisticated about all this. Right. What do I do? What in hell do I do? Because I don't think I'm anywhere near as sophisticated as I need to be . . .*

Peggy's next words, when they came at her, seemed to issue from someplace very far away, muffled, barely audible. Frances had to ask her to repeat them, and then a second time, even as they—dimly at first, then with more and more strength—began to reverberate within her.

"I said you should be terribly flattered. To have Jeff. And to have Terrence, too. After all these years . . . He still loves you, you know."

Frances stared at her.

"He finally told me why he'd looked me up, started going out with me. Because he was hoping I'd be another you."

It *hadn't* been Jeff. It hadn't been Jeff, it had been Terrence. Frances found herself sitting there, unable to speak, wondering, not knowing, which would have hurt her the more.

Peggy wasn't through. "Why do you think I was so angry with you that night at the bar? Because I was already seeing him, was threatened by you. Because he's the dearest man I've ever known. And I was beginning to sense I wasn't measuring up. To what he'd hoped for." She shook her head. "I envy you. But not in any kind of spiteful way. Because I understand. Because I think the two of you were meant for each other."

Frances began to cry. It came slowly at first, and then more quickly, until finally it was all paroxysms, great, anguished tears that flooded through her, out of her, drowning all rational thought, shattering every last one of her defenses.

Peggy ran to her and held her, pressed Frances' yielding head against her breast. "Isn't that something, kid?" she murmured. "After all these years, I finally found Mr. Right. With just a little technical flaw; he was *your* Mr. Right, not mine.

"It's probably why you took so long to get married, to find someone. Because you'd met Terrence, and found out Mom had known what she was talking about after all. There *are* those kind of men. And sometimes, if we get very, very lucky, we find them."

Frances moaned, softly, despairingly.

"I know. You're right. The luck isn't in finding them. It's in keeping them. But you could have that now. If you wanted. If you really, really want it, you can have it. He's there for you if you want him. This minute. Right now." Her voice became a tender urging. "You could go to him. You could go to him right now. Take your future in your hands. Put it all together in the way it probably always should have been. I'll take care of David if you like. Till it's all settled."

The shock of the statement stopped Frances in mid-sob. She stared at Peggy, wide-eyed.

"He loves you, Frances. I think you love him."

"No." Frances shook her head, desperately trying to regain her equilibrium. Peggy saying this, the thought of him being there . . . She saw him clearly, sitting in his apartment, sitting as if *waiting* . . . waiting for *her* . . . "No," she said again. "No, I can't do that. I never would."

Peggy ran her hand over her, patted her. "All right," she said. "I just thought I'd tell you, just in case, let you know . . ."

Frances nodded. The two sisters exchanged sad, wan smiles. The phone rang. Frances jumped up.

"Hello, Frances." It was Jeff.

"Hello."

"I'm just calling because I wanted to hear your voice. Just that. To know you're there. The rest can wait till later."

"Yes. All right." She hesitated, and looked toward her sister. "I'll probably be back when you get home.

But if not, don't worry. I'm just going over to Peggy's for a while."

She followed Peggy to her house, David in the seat behind her. At the house she got out of her car and handed David to Peggy; didn't bother going in. When Peggy and David waved good-bye, she nodded, her head lowered, not looking at them.

She drove down the small street and then turned right, toward the highway. It had been all instinct. She hadn't thought for a moment that she would do this. And then Jeff had called, which had given her the chance to tell him she'd be out of the house for a while. If he hadn't called . . . ?

Why am I doing this? She found she didn't know. Didn't know if she was prepared to throw over her marriage for him, or whether she was being driven there by something else; unfinished business, the need to satisfy the longing that had been with her all these years . . . the need to lie with him, to hold him in her arms, be held in his . . . or to simply, somehow, this time, *end* it.

She turned onto the main road and the miles began to fall away, one, two . . . She saw nothing as she drove, blind to everything on either side of her, behind her, barely noted what was ahead of her in the two lanes that made up the small highway; her unconscious taking over as she drove. Even when she had to slow because of traffic, or stop for a red light, she was barely conscious of doing it.

Terrence. After all this time. To *be* with him. Whether for forever or for just a few precious hours . . . The image of him continued to reach out to her, to blind her to everything else.

Then, suddenly, it all went awry. Her foot, pressed

hard against the gas pedal, slackened, pressed forward again, rose again, and the wagon began to slow.

Isn't this too easy?

It had come to her all at once. Peggy had had an affair with Terrence. That's what she had said. Said she had loved him. *Can a woman give up a man that easily to another woman, even her sister? Give him up after she's been rejected, found wanting? A woman scorned . . .*

No. Terrence would never scorn anyone. He had let Peggy down gently. He was a gentle man. There was no other way he could be.

And yet, even if he had . . . could Peggy—could any woman—have seen it that way? Taken even the gentlest of rejections so in stride that within minutes of leaving him for the last time she'd hand him over to her rival?

The car behind her honked; then, though it was a no-passing zone, pulled around her. Frances glanced at the speedometer. She'd slowed all the way down to forty. Ahead she saw a pull-off of some sort. She turned into it and cut the engine.

She lowered her head against the wheel. *Get control of yourself. No more paranoia. Peggy is your sister. She loves you.*

And yet . . . Her fingers, still on the wheel, tightened against it. *And yet . . . didn't she turn on me? Say all those vicious things? Can someone who loves you act like that?*

It was beginning to rain. Large, bulbous drops struck the windshield and slowly ran down it. *Yes. Of course. Peggy loves me. That doesn't mean she's not allowed to hate me, too. Besides, she'd been drinking. Remember things you've said and thought when you've had too much to drink? Things you never really meant? And yet . . .*

What if Peggy hasn't *been having an affair with Terrence? What if I was right to begin with? What if it's been Jeff all along?*

The rain was coming down harder now, the drops smaller, tighter, splattering harshly against the glass, sharp, pelting sounds echoing as they struck against the metal roof and hood. *What if all of this was a test of loyalty? Peggy showing Jeff that I would forget my husband, leave my child, rush to my dream lover . . .*

Or is there more to this? Has Jeff killed Terrence? And arranged, somehow, when I go to his place, that I'll be implicated, I'll be the one who's charged?

Unable to bear it all, she cried out, the sound of it anguished, guttural. *No. Stop thinking like this. There's no truth to any of this! It's all in your mind, tearing away at you. Some kind of nightmarish expiation of your guilt . . .*

But she couldn't keep her mind from racing.

And then the final thought hurtled at her.

What if Terrence is part *of all this? What if this has all been arranged by him and Peggy and Jeff? From the beginning . . .* Or at least since she'd first told Peggy her feelings about him? Given Peggy and Jeff a way out for the two of them?

She began to tremble, frightened for herself, for her sanity. *It's gotten so bad that now I can't trust even him . . . trust the one person who, more than anyone, represents purity to me . . .*

She switched on the engine, and then the headlights. All traces of daylight had vanished in the storm. For it was a storm now, the wind shrieking against the car, rocking it, lightning tearing at the sky, thunder booming out so loudly it seemed only inches away. The rain had become a flood, hammering at the windshield; so heavy, so rapid, that even when she shifted the wipers to high speed, they barely cleared the glass. Slowly, carefully, she pulled out of the rock-strewn area, and, her eyes straining against the sheets of rain, made as sure as she could that no one was coming, then pulled out onto the highway. Once on the road, she headed back in the direction she'd come from, toward Peggy's.

It was three miles to the turnoff. When she reached it, the storm was still raging around her. There was a car behind her, and she slowed carefully. When she turned, the car behind her turned, too.

She told herself it meant nothing, and to show that to be true, she took the first turn to the right, to allow the car to continue straight ahead. But it turned behind her.

It still doesn't mean anything. She reached the end of the small road, turned right again, toward the highway. The car behind her followed. It did the same again when she turned back onto the highway. *Maybe he's lost. Maybe there's a detour I didn't see.*

This time when she got to the turnoff to Peggy's, the car behind didn't follow her. She relaxed. Moments later, when headlights gleamed in her rearview mirror, she told herself it didn't mean anything, that it was a different car.

The rain had begun to slacken, but there was still no light; thick clouds of black screened whatever might have been left of the dying sun. Frances neared the house and looked to the driveway. Peggy's car was there. *So was Jeff's.* Frances pulled over to the side of the road across from the house, shaken. She had no idea of what to do.

There were still scattered drops of rain, distant sounds of thunder. She glanced at the car's clock, double-checking the time. Far too early for Jeff to have come home. *So maybe I'm not crazy. Maybe there was a plot. Or* . . . Her heart sank and guilt surged through her. *Maybe he was fired today. Came home for solace, came looking for me when I wasn't there* . . .

Out of the corner of her eye she saw something come at the window beside her, hit the glass. And again. This time she could make it out. It was a hand.

Instinctively her body leapt away from the door, fear constricting the cry that rose in her throat.

"Frances! Frances!"

It was Terrence's voice. Slowly, timidly, she reached over and rolled the window down a few inches. "I want to speak to you. May I?" he asked, a half shadow in the dark and rain. All of her suspicions came back . . . Peggy, Jeff, Terrence, all in this together. But his voice was the voice she'd always known, the voice of the man she'd always loved, trusted . . . "Yes," she gasped, and unlocked the door by the passenger seat.

The overhead light flashed on briefly as he flung himself into the car. In that instant she saw longing and desperation in his eyes.

His voice was tremulous, urgent; as if his whole world was within his grasp, and he knew that at any moment it might slip away. "I've been following you ever since you left your house," he told her.

She stared at him. "Peggy said you were at home."

"I was when she left. But then . . . forgive me, but I decided to try again for you. I drove to your house, but when I got near it, I saw Peggy's car. So I drove up the road a little. Figured I'd wait there till she left. But then you left together. Then when I saw you leave Peggy's without going in, saw the direction you headed toward, I hoped . . . I couldn't help it . . . I hoped that you were driving to my place. Coming to me."

She looked at him, saying nothing. The rain had increased, making the blackness outside almost impenetrable. If Jeff left Peggy's now . . . *Why is he there?* . . . It wasn't likely he'd see her.

Terrence's voice became calmer, almost resigned. "Frances," he went on, "I know I have no right to say this. But . . . all of my life, whatever I've wanted I've gotten. I don't mean easily. Most of it came hard. I had to struggle for it. But I *did* struggle. I think something that's important is worth going after, battling for." Lightning flashed, and she could see his eyes for an instant, those clear, clean eyes that still, after all these years, spoke nothing but truth.

"I don't know if she told you . . . I've been seeing Peggy. It wasn't right for me to. But I didn't realize at first . . . that I was using her, by hoping that somehow she'd be you, could take your place."

"She told me," Frances answered quietly.

She heard the breath come out of him, and there was a long silence.

"All right," he continued finally, "she told me—just enough about your marriage—to give me hope. I told you that something that's important to me is worth going after. And nothing in my life has ever been as important as you. I love you, Frances. I've always loved you."

As he said the words, she realized it was the first time he'd ever spoken them to her. And that she had never told him that she loved *him*. It had all been unspoken, *known*. But till this moment, never said aloud, never declared. She opened her mouth to speak, and then closed it again.

"So that's why I'm here," he concluded. "To tell you that I love you and that all you have to do is say the word. And David—David is part of you. I'd want him, too."

There was a flash of light from Peggy's house, and Frances turned toward it. She saw that the front door had opened. Someone was leaving . . . Jeff. Peggy was not at the door.

For several seconds neither Frances nor Terrence spoke, each watching as Jeff walked to his car, backed out of the driveway, then drove away without seeming to notice the two cars at the side of the road. When the taillights of his Toyota had faded into the distance, Frances turned toward Terrence. "I'm sorry," she told him. "I have to see my sister."

She didn't look back as she walked to the house. All of her mind was centered on what was ahead of her, on what she might find.

She rang the bell and waited. Then rang again. There was a sound of footsteps, and the door opened. Even shadowed as Peggy was from the light behind her, Frances could see. She clutched at her sister, quickly pulled the door closed behind her. "What happened?" she cried in hushed tones, looking desperately around for David.

Peggy shook her head. "He's all right. He was upstairs when it happened. I've checked him. He's still asleep." The lights of the room threw her face into full relief, completely revealed the ugly bruise below her left eye, the blood smeared across her swollen upper lip, the blood that dotted her blouse. A purplish bruise stood out on her forehead.

"He got here about an hour after you left," Peggy continued, recounting it all in a voice that echoed her expression; lifeless, dispassionate. "I tried to tell him you had just decided to take a drive. That you'd felt the need for a little time alone, away from David . . ."

"But he didn't believe you," Frances said slowly, her hand gently passing over her sister's face, as if the light, loving touch would end the pain, begin the healing . . .

"No," Peggy shrugged, her shoulders slumping. "He went into a rage . . . like nothing I've ever seen, not even from Martin . . ." She looked at Frances fully for the first time. "Anyway, he told me I was lying. Said you were having an affair with Terrence, said he knew I was covering up. Wanted me to tell him where Terrence lives."

While Peggy spoke, Frances led her into the bathroom. She found a washcloth, ran water till it was warm, then carefully, tenderly, began to wipe away the blood. Till now Peggy had been dry-eyed, but as the cloth was gently dabbed over her lip, across her cheek, small tears began to course from her eyes.

"I told him that you couldn't be having an affair with Terrence. That *I* was. He began hitting me. I wanted to scream, out of the pain, in the hope someone would hear me and stop him, but I didn't. Because of David. Jeff hit me, kept hitting me, over and over . . ."

Frances pulled her sister to her. *What have I done? What in God's name have I done?*

"Somehow I managed to get to my purse. Terrence and I had taken a picture together. I showed it to Jeff.

As far as I know, he doesn't even know what Terrence looks like. I know you never had any pictures. But somehow he seemed to believe me . . . the photo cut through all that rage. His hand was up, ready to hit me again, and then it just . . . dropped. And then he ran out of the house."

"I'm so sorry, so sorry," Frances told her. "To have got you into all of this."

Peggy shook her head. "Hey, my fault. I was the one who told you to see Terrence. And I think Jeff's going to be all right now. I think he believes me. I think all he'll feel now is shame. You should be okay."

Slowly, their arms about each other, they walked up the stairs to the room where David was sleeping. "Or do you want Jeff anymore?"

Frances, uncertain, shook her head, shrugged.

She didn't leave with David until Peggy assured her that she'd be all right, already *was* all right, that they'd speak in the morning. She didn't ask Frances where she was going.

The rain was still bad, blurring Frances' vision as she left the house. She was still uncertain. And then, as she headed down the walk, she knew. She would go with Terrence.

But when she reached the Chevy, it stood by itself. Terrence's car was gone. Despite the rain, she stood there for a moment, exposing her child and herself to it, not noticing.

Because it had come to her. *Of course.* He had more decency than she. His better judgment, his *humanity*, had given him second thoughts. There was no way, not when it actually came down to it, that he could bring himself to selfishly wreck a marriage.

Frances' lip twisted. *He was right.* Slowly coming to

herself, she did her best to wipe the rain away from David, then placed him in his little protective seat. *It's all over now. This has been an interlude. An aberration. It's all over as far as I'm concerned, as far as anything I'm going to do. It's in Jeff's hands now. I'm his wife. He's my husband. As long as he still wants it that way.*

Droplets of rain still trickling from her hair and cheeks, she headed in the direction of home.

Chapter
19

Jeff was at the car before she'd got David out of the backseat.

"I'm so glad to see you," he said, and then, as he saw David, realized. "You've seen Peggy. God, Frances, I'm so sorry, so sorry . . ."

She let him keep his arm around her as he ushered her up the porch steps and into the house.

David was half awake, and she told Jeff she'd have to put him to bed first. He nodded, a look almost like relief passing over his face, as if he welcomed, as she did, the brief time—the limbo—they'd have before they began to talk.

"David home now," David murmured sleepily as she put him into his bed and pulled the sheet up around him.

"Yes," she told him. *Home.* Is *it*? She looked about her, as she had when she'd come into the house. There was the same look to it that she'd found downstairs, on the stairway, in the upstairs hall. Something *strange* about it, unfamiliar, like something that didn't belong to her, that never had. And then as she gazed, seated at the edge of David's bed, one hand lightly touching that small form, things started to fall into place; a look of familiarity began to steal over them. After a few minutes it seemed the same as always.

Leaving David's room, she stepped out into the hallway with some trepidation. But the strangeness there was gone, too. It looked as it always had. As did the staircase, and, as she reached the foot of the stairs, as did the rest of the house.

And when she watched Jeff rise from the living room couch, she saw he was the same now, too. *Her* Jeff. Her *husband*. The man she had loved and married. The man who had given her a life that had been nearly perfect. And because it hadn't been wholly so . . .

Frances crossed to him and allowed him to enfold her in his arms. She had seen the pain on his face, understood . . .

"I'm sorry," he murmured. "I'm sorry for not trusting you. What I did to Peggy . . . God forgive me. I don't know how to make it up to her, to you . . ."

She ran her hand lightly down his arm. "It's all right. What you did to her was terrible . . . terrible, but I think she understands. I think she forgives you."

He fell silent at that, just held her and stood there with her for a very long time. Finally he released her, and, without speaking, each understanding, they began walking toward the stairs, toward their bedroom.

Once there, Jeff closed the door and drew her toward him. "I'm sorry," he said again. "I love you. I'll always love you." He kissed her, softly, tenderly. Then he kissed her again.

And then a third time, and again . . . each kiss becoming a little more ardent. She accepted his lips, allowed them, wanting to respond in kind. *He's my husband. I love him,* she told herself, trying to force the feelings, the feelings that had once come so naturally to her, trying not to show the stiffness and the lack of desire she felt.

In time he became more and more aroused, his breathing heavier, his kisses almost savage, his hands roaming her, pressing her, crushing her against him, all of him. Finally, slowly, carefully, he began to undress her.

He didn't notice her passivity, or if he did, it only served to inflame him more. Her blouse fell away, her skirt, her brassiere . . . Finally he drew down her panties, lowering himself to the floor as he did it, then kissing the length of her as he rose to his feet.

He led her to the bed and began to pull off his own clothing. Then he stopped. He drew away from her.

"Nearly forgot," he said. He went to his chest of drawers. There was a small paper bag on it. "Went out at lunch. Got this for you," he muttered, his back to her.

Turning, he came toward her. There was a tiny box in his hand. He held it out to her.

As Frances took it, he said softly, his voice barely audible, "I realize I've been wrong about a lot of things. I want to make them up to you. I guess this is kind of a symbol of that."

Standing there naked before him, she opened the box, looked down into it.

The glow of it was what she noticed first. It took a moment for her to realize exactly what it was. And then she saw. A slender, golden chain. To be worn around the neck.

She stepped back, her eyes wide.

He came toward her. "Let me put it on you."

"No." Her voice was a cry. She backed away from him.

"Please," he said, his voice still soft, pleading.

She felt the blood—her life's blood—begin to pump through her, pound at her. Nude, wholly vulnerable, she backed away. "No, no," she urged again, moaned the words. She felt her knees begin to tremble, feel as if they were about to give way.

And still he came, holding out the fragile strand of gold, raising it toward her neck.

Another step back and she found herself stopped, pinned where two walls met. This time when she tried to protest, no sound came. He was on her now, guttural murmurings coming out of him as he ran his hands across her neck, pulling at the chain as it encircled her throat.

All over. So this was the way it was to end. Never again to see David, Peggy . . . *Terrence.* Her eye fell on the sewing table. The chain was all the way around her neck now, and she felt it fasten. The large, strong hands drew slightly away, and he seemed to step back, as if before the final plunge.

It went very, very quickly. Her hand flew to the sewing table and then arced toward his body. She used every ounce of her strength, lashed out with a violence, a vehemence she'd never known.

Jeff's eyes went wide.

He stepped back, one, two steps, staring at her. A small, inarticulate sound came from his mouth. And then "Why?" he asked, and then again, "Why?"

He moved back another step, another, and then began to sway. His head was moving back and forth, unbelieving, the "Why?" formed by his lips now silent.

Then slowly, very slowly, he began to sink toward the floor.

Frances stood frozen, watching him, seeing his eyes glaze, his mouth droop open, still forming the same silent question as a thin trickle of red began to ooze from the corner of his mouth. His hands were at his stomach, nearly obscured by the blood that streamed over them, over the fingers interlaced about the thing that was staining them crimson: a pair of scissors, the gleaming steel handles the only part of them not hidden, not cloaked by blood and the flesh that enclosed them.

Chapter
20

J EFF WAS STILL ALIVE WHEN SHE CALLED TERRENCE.

His eyes were on her, the look in them unchanged as she managed to get out, "It's Frances. Please. Please come here. Now. I need you."

Terrence's response was what she yearned for. No questions, no hesitation. Just a quick "All right. I'm leaving as soon as I hang up." She didn't know if she could have handled even a single question, been able to manage another word.

Her eyes averted from the figure on the floor, she sat by the phone till she heard Terrence's car draw up. At the first sound of tires on gravel, she sprang up and ran down the stairs.

As she opened the door for Terrence, the grip she'd kept on herself till now broke. Her body fell against him, and, as the tears came, shook uncontrollably. It was a nightmare, a horror that hadn't ended. Yet with Terrence's arrival, it was a nightmare in which, for these moments, she felt wholly safe, wholly protected.

After the first rush of emotion had dwindled, Frances murmured inarticulately, then silently drew Terrence up to the bedroom. Halfway in he halted, stared at Jeff's now still and lifeless body, then at her. The sobs began again, but this time she fought through them, told him everything.

As she did, his expression changed. Noticing, she broke off instantly. Something about what she saw in his face seemed wrong. Frances stared at him, a shiver of fear quickening through her.

His look suddenly softened, and he led her gently to the bed, guided her down with him as he seated himself on its edge. His voice was gentle. "You haven't heard," he began.

A small, sick feeling stirred within her as she mutely waited for him to go on; a feeling that something had gone terribly wrong.

He wasted no time, told it to her simply and plainly. "The man who killed those women. The one who strangled them. Fastened chains around their necks. It's been on the news all afternoon. The police caught him. He's already confessed."

Frances stared at him. Despite the directness of what he'd said, somehow none of it quite connected. The words seemed to float in the air, hang there, linked to nothing; to nothing that was real. She felt dull, slow-witted, swimming through words that had no meaning; empty, hollow footprints that led to nowhere.

And then she understood. Fully. Accepted it. Very simply, very finally. No shaking of her head, no trying to negate it. Jeff hadn't murdered those women. And she had killed him, convinced that he had. Stabbed him. For no reason. For no logical reason. From hysteria. A hysteria she'd allowed to build within herself, a hysteria she'd encouraged, nurtured; a hysteria she might have cultivated because somewhere in the darkest recesses of her mind, she'd known it would lead to this, had *hoped* that it would.

When she finally spoke, her voice was drained of emotion, of all hope. "I have to call the police," she said.

"No." Terrence's response was quick, firm, unyielding.

But she shook her head, the way a very small girl would, sure of the right thing, certain that the world was all black and white, knowing that the correct thing had to be done, *must* be done. "I have to."

Terrence gripped her shoulders, his hands locking tightly around them. "You can't. You wouldn't have a prayer."

"That's not important."

"Of course it is."

"No." She turned toward the phone.

His hands were still on her shoulders, and he snapped her back toward him. Fiercely he told her, "What about David? What about your son? What would happen to him?"

David. For an instant the world stopped. She hadn't thought about him, had forgotten entirely. And then, "Peggy," she said.

He shook his head. "No good. You know that. You couldn't allow that to happen. There's no reason you should pay for this. No reason *David* should. You made a mistake. A terrible mistake. I know that. I believe you. But even if a jury believed you, too, you'd still have to pay."

Her mind was muddying again. She tried to clear it. "What else can I do?"

Terrence gestured toward Jeff. "When they find

him, if you're gone, if David's gone, it'll look as if the two of you have been abducted by whoever it was who killed Jeff."

"No," she protested. "No. It's not right."

Gently, his fingertips pressed against her lips, stilling them. "You can't think now. You're in no frame of mind to think. Let me do it for you. For you and David."

Not waiting for an answer, he rose and pulled a handkerchief out of his back pocket. Kneeling beside Jeff, he slowly, carefully rubbed the cloth over the scissors' surface. "No fingerprints," he told her. "To make it seem premeditated, calculating—not a crime of passion."

He was taking over, handling everything. Frances sat and watched him, with none of it really registering. She was able to concentrate fully on only one thing— David. Yes. She had to listen to Terrence. For David's sake. She was all he had now.

Still holding onto the handkerchief, Terrence seized a lighted lamp and turned it over, then set a chair on its side. "You struggled," he told her simply. Then, "Take only a change or two of clothing. A few things of David's." As she rose and dully picked up her purse, he shook his head. "No. Leave that behind. That would be missed, might make them wonder."

She opened a drawer, drew out a change of underclothes. There was a snapshot of Peggy in the drawer. She took that, too. After she'd found a blouse and skirt, she went into David's room. She gathered a few of his clothes, two of his toy cars, three of his little men, and handed everything to Terrence. Then she reached into the small bed and picked up her sleeping child.

He stirred drowsily, his eyes opening fully, taking in her face. Then, a shadow of contentment forming on his upper lip, he fell back asleep.

Terrence went out first, walked into the road, peered along its length, then signaled to her. Quickly she fled down the steps and into the car, huddled in the seat, David in her arms, as Terrence pulled out of the driveway. There was still no traffic as they turned down the small road and headed toward the highway.

She didn't look back. That was the old world she was leaving behind. It was a new one she was pointing to now. A new life, a life made up of herself and David and Terrence. Terrence, the man she'd yearned for for so many years. Her grip on David tightened as she shuddered.

Chapter
21

THEY GOT ONTO ROUTE 80 AND HEADED WEST.

The rain had come again, a driving, slashing rain, from a sky impenetrably black. Terrence kept the car at an almost constant fifty-five miles an hour—the legal speed limit—and twenty minutes later they crossed the Delaware and found themselves on the twisting, rising, falling, pitted Pennsylvania highway.

Terrence glanced over at Frances as she sheltered David in her arms. "It's probably too late for it tonight," he told her, "but tomorrow I'll find a car carrier for him. That would make things a little better, wouldn't it?"

Gratitude flickered through the morass that was her mind and emotions. Silently she reached her hand over and touched his arm, then withdrew it to again weave it protectively about her son.

For the next hundred miles they barely spoke, the long silence broken only twice, when Terrence asked if she needed to stop, if she were hungry. Each time she told him no.

Finally, as they neared a roadside complex of gas

stations and fast food franchises, he pulled off the highway and up to one of the restaurants. He reached into the glove compartment and took out a pair of sunglasses. "Here," he said, "better put them on. In case there's already an alert out. And do you have a scarf, something like that?"

She nodded.

"Better put that on, too. Cover up your hair as much as possible."

There was a state patrolman sitting at a booth near the entrance. She halted, felt herself faltering, and then Terrence's hand was at her elbow and he guided her past the cop, to a booth at the far end. He held David while she went to the women's room. When she returned, he asked what she wanted to eat, then went to the counter by himself.

David devoured his food hungrily, but Frances found she couldn't eat. Twice she tried, and then put the hamburger down. She looked at Terrence apologetically.

"It's going to be all right," he told her. "We'll drive until we get to Ohio. That should give us breathing space. I know a hotel there. Not likely anyone would come around looking for you there."

"Where's Daddy?"

David's voice was very loud and very clear. All the time he'd occupied himself with his small meal, he hadn't looked at Terrence once. He didn't now. *"Where's Daddy?"* he cried again, his tones high and piping. People looked around.

Terrence rose, his burger not yet finished, his cup only half drained. "We'd better go," he muttered.

"Where's Daddy?" David cried again, pushing against her as she carried him through the restaurant.

Everyone was staring at them; at David, at her, at Terrence. She felt herself stricken dumb, unable to say anything to her child, could think of no way to comfort him, distract him, quiet him, keep him from struggling in her arms.

As she stepped into the rain and dark, she began crying, unable to stop herself, averted her face from David, prayed she'd be done with her tears before they got in the car, where he'd see. What could she tell him? What could she *ever* tell him?

Hours went by, long silent hours. David had quieted down as soon as they'd got back in the car. Occasionally he had stared up at her, but never once looked at Terrence. She was nearing exhaustion when Terrence indicated a sign: Wadsworth. They were in the state of Ohio. "I know that town. Stayed there once. Good hotel. Quiet. Off the beaten track. You'll be all right there." The highway exit came up and he took it.

It was after midnight when they reached Wadsworth. When they neared the hotel, she saw it was an old one; a large frame building. She waited in the car while Terrence checked in. When they reached the door of the hotel room, he told her, "I'm going to leave you here. I've got to get back so I can be in the office tomorrow, give my notice. I'll be back, on the weekend, and the following weekend. A few days after that, we'll be able to leave here."

She stared at him uncertainly. He pulled some bills out of his pocket. "Here's two hundred dollars. That should hold you until I'm back. I've guaranteed the room with my credit card." He opened the door for her, ushered her in. "Try to stay in here. Use room service." He paused, touched her gently on the shoulder and told her, "When I come back, I'll have the car carrier." Then he left.

She turned on the television as soon as she'd put David down, pressed button after button, hoping to find a news show. But it was too late; there was nothing on but old movies and reruns of situation comedies. David seemed wide awake, was playing on the floor with his cars and men. The bed was huge, and high off the floor. "The Inn of Presidents," the sign had said downstairs. Presidents of the nineteenth century and very early twentieth had stayed here. She tried to take in the room, the bed, the braided rug, the handmade furniture, the heavy, full-length curtains, to appreciate it, all of it, to free her mind of everything else, but it wouldn't work. Everything about her felt closed in, compressed, concentrated on only the one thing—those awful moments of only brief hours before. She found herself longing for sleep, to free her of all that. Very quickly she got both David and herself ready for bed, and then climbed in with him. Swiftly, blessedly, she sank into a deep, dreamless sleep.

Chapter
22

SHE LONGED TO BUY A NEWSPAPER, PORE OVER IT, BUT Terrence had advised her to stay in the room, and she knew it was the wisest thing to do. The next few days were a small hell, as David alternated between whining about wanting to go outside and staring at her in an unsettling way, as if everything about her made him doubtful and suspicious.

Perhaps, she realized, he had reason. Wasn't *she* looking at *him* oddly, so filled with dark emotions? About what had happened. About their future. About David's reaction to it all.

Each day, constantly, obsessively, she searched the TV screen for news of Jeff's murder, of the arrest of the man she'd thought she'd killed. All the while she realized it might be in vain; it wasn't the kind of story the local shows might carry, with all their concern over area fires and politics and crime, and the network news seemed equally unlikely, its scope too wide-ranging for something that was, after all, very local news. More and more, as she found nothing, it seemed her apprehensions had been right.

Or maybe it *had* run. On one of the stations. Even on all. But perhaps only on the night she'd fled. Or even since she'd been here; brief dispatches that she missed as she anxiously checked another channel.

She longed to call Terrence, but she knew that wasn't wise. He didn't call her, probably for the same reason. *Probably.* It was in the middle of the first morning in the hotel that the thought came to her; he might not return. As hard as she tried to dismiss it, the sudden doubt wouldn't go away. What would she do then? Where would she turn? Would she give herself up? What about David?

All of which only made her yearn more desperately to call her sister. Poor Peggy. For the second time in her life to have loved ones suddenly, mysteriously, vanish from her life. What was this doing to Peggy? *I've already taken Jeff's life. Am I also destroying Peggy's as well?*

But I can't call her. Can't take the chance that the police would question her. Can't put her in the position of lying, of concealing evidence. Bad enough to do that now. *But what if I get caught? And they find Peggy knew? She'd be an accomplice. Can't call her.* Can't.

And then, almost magically, late on Friday night she was awakened by a knock on her door. She pulled it partially open. It was Terrence.

"Don't want to disturb you now. I've got a room on another floor. I'll come around in the morning," he said, and then quickly left.

He arrived early in the morning. When she let him in, she saw he had a bag in his hand. "Dye," he told her. "I think it'd be best if you changed the color of your hair."

She shut her eyes. "The papers. The news. What have they been saying?"

Terrence shook his head. "I avoided it all. No papers. Didn't turn on the radio or television. I figure it's best if we don't know anything. Might keep us from doing or saying something that . . . well, that might not be wise." He touched her tentatively. "How has it been? Are you all right?"

"Yes. No. I'm all I can be now," she told him. She picked up the dye and walked toward the small bathroom. "I'll take care of my hair now. And then, please, if we can, let's move to another place. The bed is so high. Every night I'm afraid David . . ." She didn't go on, seeing he understood.

She wore the scarf and sunglasses when they left. Her hair was dark brown now, and shorter; he'd brought scissors, too. She felt grimly, savagely grateful that he'd known enough, or been lucky enough, not to get her henna or dark black hair dyes; colors she somehow associated with murderesses.

When they reached the car, Frances found, surprised and not surprised, that Terrence had been true to his word; there in the back was the little protective seat. As she placed an unprotesting David in it, she felt something in her relax. He had returned, he had remembered about the car seat. It wasn't till that small slackening in her that she realized how tense she'd been through the nightmare of these last days. Not that it was good yet. Not that it could be good soon. It might never be that.

They didn't drive far; Terrence still had to return to work; nearly six hundred miles away. This time he found a large motel, a new, obviously prospering one. "Less likely to be paid attention to at a spot like this than at one of the small ones," he told her. But he still checked first to see if they had room service.

He arranged for their rooms—made it clear that he'd taken one separate from hers—and then, without inspecting either of them, they immediately drove off for lunch in a local mall. Later, still at the mall, she shopped for clothes for David and herself. Terrence even urged her to get bathing suits, told her he was sure it would be all right if the three of them went to the pool, now that her hair was different. "Small boys need exercise," he told her, looking at David, who promptly glanced away.

At the pool, while David played with a small water toy in the wading pond, Terrence told her, "I gave notice at work. We'll be free to get out of here in two weeks."

It was then, for the first time, that she realized what she'd done to him. Though it was already too late, she told him, "Your career. It's not right. Abandoning it just because I—" Her voice broke. ". . . Because of what I've done."

He answered her calmly, his gaze clear and certain. "It's all right. It's what I want to do. You're more important to me than anything else. Always have been." He brightened. "It'll be okay, believe me. I've got all sorts of qualifications. Jobs are no problem. And there's no rush about it. I've got savings. Enough for two years. Plus enough for the downpayment on a small house."

She shook her head. "It seems so unfair. All of this for me. And I haven't even—"

He understood immediately. "I can wait," he told her.

Late on Sunday afternoon, after Terrence had left,

Frances found herself in a kind of limbo she hadn't felt in the first hotel. Everything was too new here, too gleaming, too devoid of humanity. And she couldn't leave. She had no car; it would have been dangerous to rent or buy one in either of their names; he'd already gone over that with her.

So she was stuck here, surrounded by the inhuman furniture, the mechanical art that spread itself out on the walls, staring at the vapidities on the television set when she tried to lose herself, forget. Occasionally it was too much, and she'd walk the motel's grounds with David, or take him to the pool he loved so much. It was at the pool that she felt the most normal. It was the only place that David didn't seem lost, out of sorts, off-balance somehow. He hadn't asked for his father since that first awful night, but there were times when he looked at her that she felt the question lurking, *waiting* . . . waiting for the worst of all possible moments to be asked again.

When Terrence returned the second weekend, Frances was so grateful to see him, to feel relief from her dreadful, terrible aloneness, that she urged him to sleep with her that night.

"You're not ready for that yet," he told her, and she let it go. She knew he was right. She also didn't know if she would ever be.

The weekend wasn't good. David became impossible whenever Terrence was in the room with them; demanding, bratty, going into tantrums over nothing. She was almost relieved when Terrence said good-bye. "I'll be here Friday night," he assured her. "Then we'll be together for good." As he started to leave, he asked her, "Have you ever been in the South?"

"The South? No," she told him, surprised.

"Any relatives there? Friends you write to or call?"

"No. No one. Why?"

"Tell you next week." He smiled, kissed her tenderly on the cheek, and left.

Two days later she noticed Peggy's photo was gone.

She knew she'd taken it from home. Was sure she had had it in the hotel. Was certain she'd had it here, too. Frances looked through the drawers, over and over again, though they were so scantily filled there'd been little possibility of her missing it the first time. She searched under the bed, in the bathroom, even looked outside the door and at the grounds beyond it.

Terrence took it.

The thought, when it came, was like a blow. *He loves Peggy. Maybe always has. Maybe it wasn't till he spent this time with me that he realized* she *was the one for him, not me.*

The thought sickened her. It went beyond the idea of his not loving her, of perhaps abandoning her for Peggy, leaving her bereft, unprotected, alone in the world.

Because she *knew* him. And she knew that even if he loved Peggy, he would stick by her. Because he had committed himself to her. *Spending the rest of our lives together, me knowing, him denying . . .*

And there was the other thing. Something she never would have expected of him. The underhanded thing. Of *finding* Peggy's picture. Not just taking it, but *finding* it. How? Had he searched through her belongings? And even if not, to have taken it, to have betrayed her trust that way . . .

It can never be the same between us. The thought came hammering at her as she simultaneously railed at herself that there was no reason for her to believe he'd take it. Anything—a million other things—could have happened. It could have fallen out of the drawer, blown away, been vacuumed up by the cleaning woman. It could have fallen behind something—she pulled out all the drawers, searched the crevices, then did it a second time—*well, anyway, the odds are astronomical against Terrence's taking it.*

Of course they are. That's what makes it all so terrible.

Then that night, as she pulled back the covers, she saw it. Peggy's photograph. On David's side of the bed, the edge of it showing from under the pillow. He saw it, too. "Mine," he said possessively, and clambered into bed, where he placed the photograph against his chest.

"Did you take the picture? Did you take the picture of Aunt Peggy out of Mommy's drawer?"

David said nothing, but she saw it in his eyes.

She turned away abruptly, hiding her shame from her son. Her shame and her fear. *You've done it again. You've begun to do the same things to Terrence that you did to Jeff.*

Chapter
23

TERRENCE ARRIVED BEFORE DINNER ON FRIDAY. HE seemed happy and relaxed. "They let me go early," he told her beside the pool, where he'd found her. "Would you mind leaving now? Having dinner on the road?"

"Of course not," she told him.

"Good. The sooner we can start our life together, the better." The warmth, the *hope* in his smile, was heartbreaking.

He'd brought David several small toys; three cars, a truck, and a half-dozen plastic mechanics. David was fascinated by all of it, and played in absorption on the floor while Frances changed and got ready. On the way to the car he looked up twice at Terrence, and only after a moment of Terrence's looking back at him did he glance away.

"We're heading south," Terrence explained as they pulled out of the motel's lot. "We're going to just keep driving till we find a place that seems right. I have no links there, either," he told her. "It'll all be new to me, too. We'll be safer that way. From what I know, cops are most likely to trail you to places they figure you to head for. Towns you've lived in before. Cities with people you know. Or maybe California or New York, places people tend to head for, whether they've got links there or not."

"How far south?" she asked.

"Don't know." He smiled easily. "But how does Alabama sound to you? Seems to me we couldn't get more southern, more exotic, more hidden away."

Alabama. She hadn't a clue as to what it was like. Would it be barren, eroded, red dirt everywhere, inbred, inward people eyeing anything and anyone alien with suspicion? She glanced at Terrence and murmured, in a small voice, "All right. Alabama."

They headed toward 71, then stopped for dinner shortly after they reached it. Frances brought two of David's new toys with them into the restaurant; a mechanic and a car. As she'd hoped, they kept him engrossed during the time he wasn't eating. There was no cry of "Where's Daddy?" When two state troopers walked into the restaurant, it took a moment for her to become uneasy. When they moved off to a counter and sat with their backs to her, she almost relaxed.

On the road again, she found herself thinking she'd never been in Kentucky before. That thought ushered in another, hopeful one: *It must be getting better, for me to even think about something as mundane and innocent as that. Maybe Terrence is right. Maybe we are heading into a new life. A life where everything will be all right again.*

They stopped just outside of Louisville, and again Terrence took a separate room. "It's all right," he told her as she stared at him, guilty, hesitant. "When we have our own place. That's when we'll sleep together. And it can be only sleeping until you're ready."

The next day seemed like an augury. She prayed it was. The sky was a brilliant blue, clouds of purest white lazing through it. The temperature was comfortably cool, the breeze gentle, the sun warming. After breakfast they found themselves driving through exactly what she'd always expected to see in Kentucky, and consequently had never hoped to find—miles and miles of gleaming white rail fences edging borders of bluegrass. Blooded horses raced along the land, or stood stock-still, sunlight gracefully tracing their full-muscled bodies. David was fascinated by the horses, cried out excitedly again and again, each time pointing them out to Frances, even seeming to include Terrence in his confidence as his arm swept in one direction, then another, accompanied by his cries, again and again, of "Horsie! Horsie!"

At lunchtime they left the interstate and chanced upon a real restaurant. The food was fresh, tasty, and nourishing; the first decent meal she'd had since . . . *since I left home,* was all she allowed herself to think.

They drove through the day, stopped for dinner, then continued on. All the while the speedometer never rose more than a mile or two over the limit. She didn't ask, but was sure that Terrence was doing it for a purpose; avoiding anything that might attract a trooper's attention.

Alabama, when they finally entered it, stunned her. She'd expected ugliness. Instead it was lushly verdant. Instead of a draining flatness, there were mountains, rich with pines and other trees, many of them covered with picturesque tangles of vines. As night came on, the evening grew cool, and she realized another of her apprehensions might be swept away. She'd expected brutal, ceaseless heat. But though the day had been hot, it was now chill enough for her to pull on a sweater.

They stopped just outside of Birmingham. "I figure this is far enough down," Terrence told her. "Tomorrow we'll mosey around and see what we can turn up."

She looked at him and an odd, forgotten feeling stirred inside her. She realized it was hope.

Even David seemed different. When she put him to bed, his new toys and his old all lined up beside him, he seemed calm for the first time since that terrible day. He smiled up at her, closed his eyes and immediately fell asleep.

Breakfast was a McDonald's. "Well, civilization has reached here," Frances pointed out humorously when they spotted it; and then she realized, startled, that it was the first humorous thing she'd said since . . . *since that day*. She wasn't sure, but the feeling that erupted at that realization, and that she fought instantaneously, successfully, to keep down, seemed to have been shame.

"Anniston," Terrence said as they began driving and neared a sign. "I've heard of that somewhere. Let's head in that direction."

They reached Anniston, a sprawl of fast food places and equally ugly malls, but they drove through it, and soon came to a small town with a square that the road meandered around. The buildings that lined each side of the square were all small, and old, but well kept-up. There were trees along the sidewalks, and crowds of flowers, golden, red, pink, white. They surrounded a

Civil War monument in the center of the square itself. "Home?" Terrence asked.

Home. The word made Frances shudder. But she gave him a small nod, and as much of a smile as she could muster. "Could be," she told him. She concentrated on the seeming peace of the place, tried not to dwell on its total foreignness, tried not to think at all of what home had once meant to her.

Terrence circled the square and headed back toward Anniston. Halfway there, he pulled up at a motel. "Our headquarters," he told her. "Tomorrow I go looking for a house."

"And a job?"

"We're okay. We'll be okay for a long time, remember?" he told her, and then as the doubt remained in her eyes, he smiled. "But if there's time, I'll look for that job, too."

The motel was depressing, with mild seediness added to the usual dehumanization. But she did all she could to make the best of it, and three days later Terrence called her, very excited. "I have a job in Anniston; a drafting job with a real chance to move into design. And I think I've found the place for us. I'll be over in a few minutes."

The house was two blocks from the square. It was small and brick and very tidy. The grounds were manicured, dotted by small pines, and the inside was in perfect shape. The kitchen was a good size, and the appliances no more than a few years old, each immaculately maintained. There was an enclosed yard that was the perfect size for David. The other homes on the street wore their own air of being cared for. The price was stunningly low. "Yes," she told Terrence, and he beamed.

The owners already had a retirement home they were eager to move into, and were delighted that Terrence and Frances wanted to buy their furniture, too. Three weeks later she and Terrence and David moved in.

That night, for the first time ever, she and Terrence slept together. They had a corner bedroom, with one side overlooking the yard, and the other screened by a huge magnolia. When, quiet and serious, he came to bed, she encouraged him to make love to her. First, very sweetly and simply, he asked what she liked and didn't like, and she found it easy to tell him.

He was tender and patient, and in the end, full of matched passion; their lovemaking was all she could have hoped it would be, the way things were. He fell asleep almost immediately, and she soon after.

That evening was when Frances had her first nightmare.

She awoke from it with a start, eyes wide open, heart pounding, body pouring cold sweat. Immediately she glanced at Terrence, terrified that her scream in the dream had been real as well, and that he had heard. But he was sleeping peacefully.

They came every night after that, and each time she reacted the same way; glancing at Terrence, afraid that this time he'd know; that the happiness and contentment he felt about their life together was unshared.

He had done all he could to make things easy for her. Even before they'd moved in, he'd prepared a "bible" for her; a history of their lives should anyone ask questions of them, so they'd have their stories straight, so no one would begin to suspect anything. They had met in New York while she was living in

Brooklyn and both were working in Manhattan; they'd been married four years. She'd always hated cold weather, and, for no explainable reason, had always been attracted to Alabama; coming here had felt like coming home. Terrence, the narrative went on, had been lucky in that he had the capabilities of working virtually anywhere, and so they'd driven here and by chance found what they considered the perfect spot; this last a response certain to please the natives.

From the first day she was grateful for the bible. The neighbors were immediately friendly—and inquisitive. The questions never seemed to stop, and despite all the answers she was able to give them quickly, easily, she had the feeling that somehow she wasn't satisfying them. It seemed to her that more and more their faces were masks of suspicion.

It's only your damn paranoia, your guilt, she told herself, *like the nightmares. It's all in your mind, that's all it is.* But no matter how often she forced herself to think it, it did no good. She began picking times to leave the house when she didn't think the neighbors would be around, and sometimes didn't answer the doorbell when they came to call. She felt herself becoming more and more furtive, and wondered if the looks she got from them when they did meet were what she thought; looks of dark skepticism, of ever more deepened suspicion.

She couldn't bring herself to talk to Terrence about any of this. He seemed so happy, so delighted to be with her. He left for work at the last minute, returned as quickly as he could. Subtly, without pushing it, he tried to win David over, but though her son—her son and Jeff's, she sometimes found herself thinking—would eagerly grab up whatever new toys Terrence brought him, the change she thought she'd seen in him, the change she'd hoped for, seemed not to have happened. He tended to avoid Terrence, to not respond when Terrence spoke to him. He absolutely would not allow Terrence to read to him, and if Terrence sat next to him on the couch, he would move away after a moment or two.

There wasn't a single night that the nightmares didn't come; they were full of blackness and terror, a petrifying, nameless horror that, once awake, left her gasping for breath. She began trying to put off sleep; going to bed with Terrence, then fighting to remain awake, trying to forestall the bottomless terror that would leave her bathed in icy perspiration. Making it all worse was her fear that Terrence would find out, would have his perfect world shattered, discover that nothing had healed, nothing at all.

Chapter
24

IT WAS ON A WEDNESDAY MORNING, TWO MONTHS AFTER they'd moved into the house, when the horror stopped being confined to the night.

She'd checked to be sure no one was outside, then left with David to go shopping. But at the local supermarket she bumped into Lonnie Mae Cleaver, a young neighbor from two houses down. Frances smiled at her, tried to brush past, but Lonnie Mae was obviously eager to talk.

"Did you hear?" she asked, excitement in her voice and eyes.

Frances waited, trying not to show impatience.

"About what happened down to Oxalla, I mean."

"No," Frances told her, looking at her list, hoping the quick glance would tell Lonnie Mae that she was busy and end the conversation.

But Lonnie Mae said, "Linelle Oakes. I went to the high school with her. Last night, they found her body."

Frances stared at Lonnie Mae. She obviously wasn't

through. *At least,* Frances told herself, grateful for it, *she's not asking any questions.*

Then all the gratitude fled.

"Stripped naked she was. Not a stitch on her. Except for some old necklace, or something. Choked to death, is what they said it was."

Lonnie Mae continued talking, but Frances heard none of it. Every part of her had suddenly chilled. Numbness clouded her mind. Eventually, when Lonnie Mae seemed to be done, Frances blindly resumed her course through the store's aisles. Over and over again she had to remind herself of what she needed to buy, over and over found herself staring, a can or a package or a bagful of something in her hand, staring at it as if she had no idea of what it was; sometimes she replaced it, finally realizing it was nothing she needed or wanted.

Somehow she got through the checkout line, managed to offer the necessary money, found her way to the car and drove unseeingly home.

She had the car's radio on, but there was no news on it, no matter what station she tried. The moment she entered the house, she turned on the kitchen radio, listening as she dazedly put away the groceries. Oxalla was two towns away. It had its own station, and she kept the radio tuned to it. It was nearly eleven. And then eleven, and the news came on.

It was the lead story. Linelle Oakes, twenty-seven. Found strangled in the woods outside Oxalla. All she had on was her school ring, her wedding and engagement rings . . . and a golden chain about her neck. Frances snapped the radio off and sank into the nearest chair.

Terrence. It has to be.

His disappearance from high school. Of course. It was already happening then. He'd been sent to reform school, to a mental institution or hidden away by his parents. Of course.

First New Jersey, now here. It has to be. All his care in coming here; his driving at the speed limit; his choice of that first hotel. His not making the mistake of renting a car in either of our names. Being so aware of where a fugitive would be looked for. Knowingly choosing the least likely place. The history of our lives that he drew up; beautifully detailed, not a hole in it that people could seize on, tear at. Not once had all those questioning neighbors caught her in anything that didn't add up. *Because of Terrence's care.*

How unusual to have been so thorough, so absolutely perfect. She'd not even thought about it. Why should she have, when everything about him was so highly competent? But now . . . how could it have come so easily to him, so naturally . . . unless he had done it before? To protect *himself.*

And the other thing. The worst of them all.

He had been away two nights ago. A business meeting in Birmingham, he'd told her. Had even called her from there that evening. Or *said* that was where he was calling from. Terrence had killed all those women. There was no other explanation.

Swiftly she found a bag and began throwing things in, suddenly afraid of lingering one extra moment. In David's room she filled another bag, made sure, despite her rising fear, that she'd collected enough of his beloved toys. She ran out to the car, threw the bags in, then returned for David.

In the car she fumbled with the keys, forgot to feed in the gas. Her heart was beating wildly. At any moment Terrence could suddenly return, find her, realize she *knew* . . .

And then the engine turned over, and she quickly drew out of the driveway, then turned and headed in the direction opposite from the one Terrence would take if he were coming home.

She took one of the small roads out of town; avoided the highway on the chance that when he found her missing, he'd try to pursue her. From time to time she'd turn off onto a new road, always, as best she could tell, vaguely heading due north.

Two hours later she stopped at a gas station. It was open, and at the far end of its drive there was a phone booth. David was asleep. As the car was being gassed up, she went to the phone. She got the number of the Anniston police and called.

The call was upsetting. The cop on the other end kept insisting that Frances give her name. It was almost as if he weren't listening to what she was telling him, wouldn't certify it as anything till he knew who was calling. But she persisted, told him again and again of her suspicions, hammered it at him. Finally, drained, still refusing to give her name, afraid the call would be traced, she hung up. She'd done all she could.

Chapter
25

DAVID AWAKENED EARLY. THE MOTEL SHE'D FOUND THE night before had a pool. After breakfast she let him play in it for as long as he wanted, hoping it would dispel some of his energy; make him more agreeable to a long ride.

Late in the morning they crossed into Tennessee. In Fayetteville she found a bank. Terrence had provided her with a credit card. She drew out all the cash she could on it. Two thousand dollars. She'd taken another two hundred from the house.

There was a possibility that Terrence, if he hadn't been picked up, might find out about the bank transaction. She backtracked forty miles, then headed west. After another hundred miles she turned north. Toward Iowa. She'd never been there. She'd never mentioned Iowa to Terrence, he'd never mentioned it to her. She was using his own thinking now. She'd go to Iowa. Once there, she'd . . . what? She had no idea, felt her mind go blank. David, this car, their clothing, his toys, and almost twenty-two hundred dollars. That was her entire world now, a world cut loose from its moorings. With a grimace, she tightened her grip on the wheel. She'd drive to Iowa. When she got there it would be time enough to figure out what to do, hope that something presented itself.

She drove through the flatlands of Missouri, with its small houses and suggestions of marginal poverty. Then into Illinois and at last into Iowa, three days after she'd started. Hours later she had found her new home.

Ottumwa. A small city, one that gave the impression of edging into oblivion. Humid. But the apartment in the three-story brick building was cheap. Two rooms, furnished, for $285. David was fascinated by it, explored it over and over again. There was a floor-level cubbyhole on a wall in the living room. He was enchanted when she told him it was for his toys. For days he happily put them in and took them out. At night before bed he scrambled around the drably decorated room, picking his things up and putting them away. "David's," he'd say, pointing, and she never knew whether he meant the toys, the cubbyhole or both.

There'd been nothing on the car radio or in the newspapers about Terrence or a second murder while she'd traveled; there was nothing here, either. She tried to convince herself it was like before; events in out-of-the-way places would generate little interest elsewhere. She refused to allow herself to think beyond that. She was hidden away. She was safe. Frances told herself that forcefully, over and over, till it was nearly a belief. *Nearly*.

Her landlord had asked for two months' rent in advance. After she'd paid it and counted up what was left, she had nearly fourteen hundred dollars. Enough to get along on for a while. But sooner or later she would have to work, would have to leave David. The way her mother had done with her. The way Frances had vowed she never would.

Before her marriage she had had an assortment of jobs. Babysitting and sales-clerking in high school; more of that and movie house ticket-selling and assisting a veterinarian during her college days. After graduation she'd been fooled by two successive "administrative assistant" jobs: she'd been a Gal Friday each time, with no prayer of advancement. After that, she'd worked as a stockbroker, the job she'd had when she met Jeff. She'd been adequate at it, but never more than that, had never really liked it. It had been a job, nothing more.

A first glance at the Ottumwa classifieds told her it didn't make any difference; no openings for stockbrokers here. Not even for administrative assistants of any stripe. Few ads showed the salaries; from her experience an indication of dismal pay. After that, daily searches of the paper showed no improvement. Sales jobs that blithely promised the world, work-at-home employment that offered just as unlikely opportunities. Past that, very little else. After three weeks Frances was resigned. She'd find something, anything, as long as it offered enough to let her get by.

In those weeks she'd made friends of a sort with Mr. and Mrs. Miller; she never learned their first names. Mr. Miller was the building's custodian. He was old— possibly even into his late seventies—too old for such work, very thin and stooped, with hollowed cheeks and a faintly bemused manner. He spoke little, but his eyes were kind. Mrs. Miller, short and thick-bodied, seemed younger than her husband, but just barely. Sometimes she helped him when he put out the garbage. Most of the time she sat outside on the worn, cracked sidewalk, in a folding wooden chair. She had an accent of some sort, and had a disconcerting way of speaking; her words were clipped and jumped out at you like small explosions. But she doted on David, and brightened whenever she saw him. "*Such* a little boy, *such* a little boy," she would exclaim over and over.

"I need to get a job," Frances told her one afternoon. "I need to find some work, and I need a person who can take care of David while I'm away. Someone I can trust." It was obvious the Millers were barely getting along. David liked both of them. Perhaps . . .

"The factory three blocks away needs assemblers," Mrs. Miller shot out in her direct, abrupt manner. "It's good money. You could leave the boy here. I charge you two dollars an hour. Give him food for nothing. He's little. He don't need much."

The "factory" turned out to be a one-story building, not much bigger than a diner. There was no air-conditioning, and the lighting was poor. The job paid $4.55 an hour. Very small, very intricate plastic parts had to be fitted together. Quickly. Frances turned it down. Two weeks later she went back. A night slot was available. She could start the next day. She took it. When she got home, Mrs. Miller quickly agreed to drop to a dollar and a half.

The hours were from midnight to eight-fifteen in the morning. Ideal, really, Frances told herself half seriously. She was able to confine her sleeping to David's naps and after she'd put him to bed at six-thirty. On weekends Mrs. Miller would volunteer to take David for an hour or two. "You don't need worry money," she would say, waving her hand and shaking her head. Then Frances would collapse on the small fold-out couch in the living room that she slept on; she'd given David the bed.

Her life became very small, and very circumscribed. She rarely used the car, not wanting to waste money on gas. The apartment, work, occasional sorties to shops for the bare necessities, books from the library for her and David, conversations of sorts with the Millers when she dropped him off or picked him up, and during the other times she ran into them. The other tenants did no more than nod to her, nor she to them. They were a grubby lot, uniformly morose. Occasionally she could hear fights in the other apartments between husband and wife, parents and children. Sometimes there were loud, unexplained crashes. But it was all right; it never went beyond that. No apparent drugs, no thefts, no real violence.

At work there were occasional, unpleasant passes from the men who came and went. But mostly they were abortive; something in her manner made them back off. She had no idea what she was doing, but she was grateful for whatever it was.

More disturbing as time went on were the religious pamphlets. They began arriving in the mailbox the middle of the second week. Frances paid little attention at first; just something in the box, like the occasional circular or letter addressed to "Occupant."

It took a few days for her to realize they weren't part of the mail; there was no address on them, no stamp. Not surprising. This, after all, was the Bible Belt. Someone was merely being hopeful. But on a day when the mail hadn't yet been delivered, Frances noticed that there was nothing behind the glass doors of the other mailboxes; only hers. She took the leaflet out and for the first time read a few words.

It was what she'd expected; fundamentalist stuff; hellfire and damnation. She could only get through the first two paragraphs. Once in the apartment, she crumpled it and threw it away. But as the days went on, slowly, so slowly at first that she didn't even notice it, the uneasiness began.

Always in her mailbox, never in the others. She was being singled out. Someone had decided she was damned.

Frances didn't go to church. She never had. She wasn't religious. Obviously someone had noticed. Mr. and Mrs. Miller. Who else? But she shook her head. *Not them. It couldn't be them. They're kind, decent people.* Or did it even have anything at all to do with churchgoing and the religious? Was it something else? *From* someone else?

Terrence.

The thought was absurd, and she told herself it was, treated it that way. But the suspicion wouldn't go away. Terrence had found her. The twisted part of him was showing, torturing her, lying in wait . . .

Then one morning it got worse. She came home and, as she moved to the front door, saw there was nothing in the box. She opened it to be sure. Empty. *Maybe it's over.* She sagged a bit, hoping it was so, fearing the hope would be shattered. She hurried up the stairs to the Millers', knocked on their door. "Shh," Mrs. Miller told her when she opened the door. "The boy is still asleep."

He didn't waken as she gathered him protectively into her arms. When she fumbled for her keys, he stirred only slightly. Frances unlocked the door and opened it. As she did, she glanced down at the floor. There it was. Lying on the floor, inches from her feet.

Another pamphlet. This one had something scrawled on it.

Quickly she brought David into his room and laid him down on his bed, praying he'd sleep just a little longer. Pushing back her dread, she hesitantly returned to the living room. Eyes averted, she picked the thing up. She insisted to herself she would throw it away without looking. But she couldn't help herself.

It was just one word, crudely lettered, in pencil. R E A D, it said. Each letter was capitalized, each was individually underlined.

She stood there and read it, her heart beginning to thud wildly. It was about the sins of the fathers being visited upon the children. The fathers; interchangeable with *parents; mothers.* The children: *David. No. Stop it. It means nothing. You're only thinking this because of all that's happened. Leave it alone.* Ignore it.

But she couldn't. Yes, it was probably some poor soul, trying to make the world live the way *he* lives, sure it's the only way. *Trying in his misguided way to help me. That's all.*

And yet . . .

Before, it had been the mailbox. Now it had been slipped under her door. It had become invasive. And that handwritten urging, the formation of the letters primitive, the insistence of the word somehow threatening . . .

As the days wore on it grew worse. Always waiting for her as she opened the door. Always with a penciled urging. T A K E N O T I C E. H A R K E N. And the one that chilled her, B E F O R E I T S T O O L A T E. She found herself sobbing as she crumpled it and threw it away, refusing to read it, to read any more, to feel the words stabbing at her . . .

Guilt. Damnation. Sin. The words kept battering at her, threatening to sunder the wall she'd built up in herself; the all-necessary wall that held back the horror of what she'd done to Jeff. To think about that, to recognize, fully recognize, what she'd done, allow herself to dwell on it . . . it would destroy her, drive her mad. She couldn't give way to that. She was all David had. He needed her. Desperately. She had to fight, not allow herself to give way.

She tried to live normally. On David's second birthday the Millers agreed to attend his little party. Frances had made a cake and bought ice cream, party hats, and noisemakers. A set of plastic men, two plastic cars, a truck and two picture books were the presents she gave him. The Millers handed him a dollar and a little book. David seemed stunned by the bountifulness of it all. For weeks after, he delighted in jabbering about the party and his becoming two, his eyes bright as he recounted all the details.

But how could she make it normal, keep it that way? When she came home in the morning, when she left at night, despite her determination to dismiss it, to convince herself she was making something out of nothing, she couldn't keep from *watching* as she walked, watching for something, someone, who would suddenly step out of the shadows and . . .

One day she found David sitting on the floor by the garbage can near the stove. He had pulled something out of it. His eyes were wide.

Some of the pamphlets had been in the form of black and white comic books, the drawings stark and fevered. This was one of them. Frances fought to keep her voice calm as she asked David if she might see it. He handed it to her.

It was one of the worst: sinners being consumed by flames, tortured by demons. Sadism oozed from it. Madness crouched at its edges. David was looking up at her expectantly, waiting to get it back. His eyes were large and gleaming.

"This isn't for little boys," she told him. "This is just silly stuff. That's why I threw it away." Very calmly she put it back into the trash, picked him up and carried him to the couch, where she read him a story, tried to assure herself that he had believed her, had forgotten all about the drawings, been unaffected by them. Later, after she'd put him to bed, before she lay down herself, she went to the wastebasket, tore the pamphlet into very small pieces and made sure they were shaken down below the rest of the trash.

And then, three weeks later, as she was giving him his bath, he said it.

He was moving a little plastic boat around in the water, not looking at her. "I don't want to be a little boy anymore."

"Why not?" Frances glanced down at him, puzzled, wondering. The hand that had been scrubbing him became still.

"Because sinners take little boys and throw them in fire and they eat them."

All of the world seemed to be crowding in on her, crushing her. The silence of the room became overwhelming. Then he looked up at her, and as their eyes met, he began to cry, and then wail, throwing himself at her. She seized him, pressed his dripping body against her, held him tight, told him it was all right, that it wasn't true, that he would always be safe, that all children would be . . .

Finally he was calm again. It required everything in her to gather her courage. She would give anything to keep him from thinking about it again. But she needed to *know*. "Who told you that? Who told you that silly old story?" She looked away, so he couldn't see the wildness and fear in her eyes.

"Mrs. Miller. She always tells me that."

Mrs. Miller. Not a strange man in a playground. Not Terrence. Mrs. Miller, telling David stories, leaving her little pamphlets . . . Mrs. Miller. *The woman I entrusted my son with.*

That was over. All over. Had to be. From this moment. Instead of dressing David in his pajamas, Frances put him in a fresh set of street clothes. He looked at her with interest.

"We're going on a trip. Mommy and David are going in the car on a long trip. We're going home."

Home. To what was left of home. To Peggy. Frances packed hurriedly, anxious to be away from here. It had been almost eight months. If Terrence had somehow escaped any problems with the law and had sought her out, he'd long ago have tried to find her in New Jersey, would long ago have given up. *Wouldn't he?*

She wrote a note and, as she left, taped it to the Millers' door. "We've had to leave. Thank you for taking care of David. Frances." The woman was a monster, but she hadn't known. She'd tried to do what she thought was best.

Frances had no phone in her apartment. She didn't seek one as she drove away. She had no plan to call Peggy. Because there was always that chance. The chance that in the few days before she got there, Terrence would arrive at Peggy's door. Perhaps for the first time, perhaps not. If Peggy knew she was coming, she would have to lie, perhaps give herself away.

I can't take that chance. I have to live this way, think this way. I'll have to live this way forever. Always. Unless a day comes when I know I'm safe.

Chapter
26

It was late on a Thursday night, nearly nine, when Frances reached Peggy's. The night was so dark that until she pulled up alongside it, she didn't see there was an unfamiliar car in the driveway. *Maybe a date.* Suddenly she had misgivings about not having called in advance. To arrive this way, unannounced, with a man there, maybe someone important to Peggy, someone she wanted to be alone with . . . But Frances was too tired and rocky to dwell on it. She had driven more than six hundred miles since morning.

David had awakened when they stopped. He stared at her drowsily as she picked him up, then fell back asleep during the few short steps to the front door. As she rang the bell, Frances sagged against the door-frame. She felt she couldn't have gone another mile.

The inner door opened and Peggy stood there, blankly staring into the blackness of the glass storm door. "Yes?" she asked, as Frances felt overpowering emotion surge through her.

"It's me. It's Frances. I'm . . . we're back."

Peggy rushing at her, embracing her, sobbing.

Clutching her, asking where she'd been, how she was, not listening, too overwrought, seizing David, pressing him to her, covering him with kisses . . . And then retreating a few steps and turning, looking at someone in the room just off the hall.

He was standing there, watching it all, motionless. *Jeff.*

Frances staggered, tried to support herself against an end table, heard candlesticks and glassware tumbling to the floor . . .

And then she was lying on the couch and he was crouching over her. His eyes were tender and searching. "Frances, are you all right?" He said it over and over again, patiently trying to break through.

She stared up at him, unable to speak.

Jeff indicated the kitchen. "She's gone to get water," he whispered. He shook his head slightly, as if to warn Frances, forestall her. "She doesn't know." There was a pause, and just as she heard her sister's steps coming toward them, he finished, "Doesn't know what you did. No one does."

What you did. Frances felt herself beginning to shake. She tried to still it, pressed down against the cushions, tried to force it away, but it only got worse. When she tried to take the water, her hand was trembling so much Peggy softly said "No," and tried to put the glass to her lips. But she was shaking too much even for that.

Frances turned away, shaking her head. "No. That's all right. I'll be all right."

She heard Peggy rise and say to Jeff, "She needs to be with you. I'll put David to bed."

Then Jeff's hand was on her brow. His touch was gentle. "Take it easy, babe. Take it easy. You'll be all right." His voice was a soft urging, as if he were *willing* her to be all right.

She turned and looked at him, lifted herself partway up against the couch. When she tried, she found again that she couldn't speak.

Jeff nodded. He understood that she wanted to know. Had to be told. "You thought I was dead. I know. I was conscious all the time. Heard you on the phone. Heard the guy come in. Heard the two of you talking. Even then, even when it was happening, I understood what you'd done. Stupid of me . . . I'd never thought . . . Those murders . . . the chain . . . I'd forgotten about all of that."

Jeff shook his head, tenderly brushed a lock of her hair back from her face. His expression was tired, sad, resigned. Yet it suggested a flickering hope. "You were both so anxious to be together, you couldn't think of me as anything but dead."

The words were like a force that struck her, stunned her so deeply that it was only by degrees that she felt the shame beginning to filter through. Truth coming at her like a bludgeon, but truth all the same . . . She found she couldn't look at him.

But there was no malice in his tone. "It was all right. Even when I was lying there, thinking it was all over. It was all right. I understood. I'd left you alone too much, alone with no one nearby, and then those murders . . . Unsettling, all of it . . . and then for him to come along . . . someone who I guess was able to offer you more in some ways than I ever could."

Terrence. She shook her head violently as she thought of him, doing all she could to force away the memory. She tried to speak, but he lightly touched her lips, shook his head.

"Not now. There's nothing to say. Later, when we're home."

Home. Dread flooded through her. "No!" she cried. "No! I can't go back there!" Instantly that single word had leveled all the walls, the walls she'd desperately created to keep from facing the enormity of what she'd done. "No! No, I can't!"

Jeff's voice remained quiet, reassuring. "No, of course not. Not there. Or course not there. I rented an apartment. After I got out . . ." He interrupted himself, avoided saying "hospital," as if to keep from calling attention to what she'd done to him. "It's not very big. But it's big enough. I rented one big enough for three. Just in case. In case someday . . ."

That was when she fell into his arms and allowed it to all come out, all the months of fear and shame and loss, sobbed as she hadn't since she'd been a very little girl.

He waited, held her till she was done. Then he cupped her chin with his hand, studied her, assured himself that she could handle things now. Satisfied, he said, "I'll tell Peggy we're leaving. She can bring David to us in the morning."

When they reached the apartment, he had to carry her in. She had fallen asleep, a deep, dreamless sleep of utter exhaustion.

Chapter
27

It was odd how things fell back into place. Or nearly so.

David joined them in the apartment the next morning, and they were a family again. Husband, wife, child, living together. David had forgotten Jeff, yet there seemed to be some residue of memory. He allowed Jeff to be affectionate with him almost immediately. Within a few days he began seeking him out to tell him things, or climb all over him as he sat reading the paper.

The lovemaking began on the second night. She found to her surprise she was able to respond, at least on a physical level. She had been deprived for a long time, and it showed in her virtually instant reaction to his caresses.

He called the company and arranged for an immediate week off. She appreciated his doing that. She needed all the help she could get with the reentry.

"I never told the police," he had told her on that first morning together. "All I said was that it came so suddenly. A knife flashing at me as I entered the bedroom, before I turned on the light. So quickly that I never saw who it was. Because I didn't want anything to happen to you." His eyes had teared as he'd said this, and then he added, "The time those kids—or whoever it was—trashed the house . . . it made it easier for the detectives to understand, to not really question anything."

He had loved her that much. Understood her on so deep a level. She had begun apologizing to him even before they'd reached the apartment, but he'd cut her short. "Please don't talk about it," he'd told her. "I understood. That's over with now. All that counts is our life together. What we had before, what we have ahead of us. The three of us."

She tried, on a far lesser level, to reciprocate. But despite herself the thoughts would creep into her mind, practically from the beginning.

She had gone to Peggy's and he had been there.

Nothing wrong with that. They were two bereft people, related by marriage, far from all their former friends, comforting each other. It was understandable; even necessary. And if there had been something more . . . Wasn't that understandable too? And even if not, how could she, after what she'd done, to Jeff, with Terrence . . . how could she feel in any position to cast blame?

And yet . . . He had been at Peggy's that night. Had some of his clothing been there, too? There was a suit of his missing. Some shirts, a couple of ties . . .

She asked him about the suit once, hating herself for it, but unable to keep from doing it. His reply was offhand, even humorous. "Oh, right. You should have seen what I did to that one. On a construction site in Massachusetts. Caught the jacket on a machine and ripped out the entire side. Then I was scrambling down a hill, slipped, and lost the left knee. Had to dump it there and buy a whole new one."

She didn't ask him about the shirts or ties. They could have worn out, become soiled, or simply lost when he moved. That's what she told herself, and she was sure it was so. And yet . . .

One night some weeks later she steeled herself enough so that she could ask, "That night. What Terrence said. Of course he made it up; about the man confessing, I mean."

But Jeff had shaken his head. "Just one of those coincidences. A guy really did. Later on they found he was just some kind of loon; the type who likes to go around confessing to all sorts of things."

So Terrence hadn't lied. Not that it made any difference, of course. And yet . . . How odd that it shook her as much as it did. One honest statement in a web of lies; what difference could that one thing make? Why should it make any at all? And yet, somehow, it did . . .

She yearned for therapy, for help of some kind. This time, there'd be no problem with money. Jeff's old boss was gone, there was a new one who loved his work, and there'd been a sizeable raise. But she dreaded the thought of talking to a stranger about all that she had done, to expect him to treat her as a rational human being. It seemed ludicrous, impossible. Instead, she talked to Jeff as much as she felt she could, got all of it out that she could, tried to busy herself with her life, with David.

She yearned to talk to Peggy about it. To get it all out in the open. Everything. But it seemed too awful to tell anyone; her trying to kill Jeff, her leaving with Terrence.

Instead, Frances had told Peggy she'd been abducted by a stranger, imprisoned by him, until one day he'd disappeared. "Have you told the police? Have they caught him?" Peggy asked that first time, and then, more and more maddeningly, each time they were in touch with each other. At times Frances felt she couldn't take any more of it; any more lying, any more assuring Peggy that the police were doing all they could, that they'd let her know if he was found. To tell her all of it, to spill out this sickness in her, the sickness that couldn't let the idea go of Peggy and Jeff as lovers . . . After she'd gone off with Terrence, *maybe even before* . . . How cleansing that might be. Or totally destructive.

Somehow she managed, led what to all appearances was a normal life. She did the shopping, the cleaning; she read, watched television with David and Jeff, swam, picnicked. News shows and papers were a little harder. The occasional rape story, the occasional disappearance of a woman . . . Nothing like before, but sometimes they seemed too reminiscent.

It was while doing one of those normal things—driving along the highway into the next town to buy material for an outfit she was making David—that she drove past the road that led to their old house. A car was waiting to pull out of that road as she approached. The August sun was behind her, and full on the driver's face.

It was Terrence.

There was no mistaking him. No mistaking his car. Abruptly she turned her head away as she went by him, hitting the gas. As she passed him, her eye went immediately to the rearview mirror. No. It was all right. He was turning in the opposite direction. Nevertheless, she kept glancing into the mirror, making sure.

Once, as she stared, her eye fell on David, who was in the car seat behind her. He noticed, and smiled back at her into the mirror; there was nothing in his expression that indicated he'd seen Terrence. He was three now, and aside from his natural brightness seemed like any boy of his age; full of energy and blessedly normal. Normal despite all that had happened. All that had happened and that she had hoped was all over. And now . . . *to see him again*. She shuddered, and once again glanced into the rearview mirror, an act she repeated all the way home.

The phone was ringing as she entered the apartment. It was Jeff. He called twice a day now, a thoughtful gesture; checking in, keeping in touch. Never had she felt more grateful. She told him, and felt the relief flood through her as he said, "I'll call the police. And I'm telling Fred I need another two weeks. If I can, I'll begin it as soon as I've spoken to him. I'm not leaving you alone. You need me there."

Chapter
28

NOTHING HAPPENED. THE POLICE DIDN'T FIND TERRENCE, and she didn't see him again. After two weeks Jeff returned to work and all seemed normal. So normal that one Saturday she decided to drive by their old house. It would be the first time since she'd come back. She felt she could handle it now.

She turned off the highway onto the narrow country road. She was alone; Jeff was minding David. She hadn't told him where she was going.

The tiny town just off the highway seemed unchanged. She passed the crossroad, then glanced up and to the left as she went by Mrs. Emenesky's place. It, too, looked the same as ever.

But her old house didn't.

Frances had intended to simply drive by. Instead, she slowed and then stopped, bewildered. *No one was living here.*

It was immediately apparent. The grass hadn't been cut all summer. The driveway was empty and choked with weeds. The bushes were overgrown, untrimmed. The curtains in the windows hadn't changed. She felt herself falter; the unexpectedness of this, the shock of it. Then, determinedly, she gunned the engine, swerved into the driveway, braked, slammed into reverse, sped back out, then headed back to the apartment. To Jeff, to what she prayed would be an explanation that didn't unsettle her further.

He read her expression as soon as she came home, silently held her, then encouraged David to watch a children's show on television. When he came back to her, he gently encouraged her to tell him what was wrong.

"I'm sorry. I suppose I should have told you," he said when she was done. They were in the apartment's small kitchen. He rose and walked toward the window. He looked out for a moment, and then turned to her. "I couldn't sell it. Not at the beginning. It had been our world. *My* world. Because it was ours. I just couldn't do it. It would have been too . . . final. I couldn't sell it for the same reason that I got this apartment, one that was big enough for all of us. In case . . ." His voice trailed off. "I should have told you, but somehow the time never seemed right. After you came back, I thought maybe when this place felt more like home. Or we found a new house." He came back to her, took her hands in his. "Well, I guess it is time now. I guess it's time to sell it."

Frances stared at him. She saw the look in his eyes. Finally she said, "No. We're going back."

"You don't mean it."

"Yes." She said it simply, firmly.

"Please don't do it for my sake."

"I'm not. You're right. That was our world. It should be again."

A month later they moved back in. Jeff had urged

her over and over to reconsider, afraid of what memories it might stir. But she was adamant. It would be as if nothing had happened; as if nothing had interrupted their life together. It would be a refusal to allow anything to scar them, deter them.

True, there were thoughts of Terrence, of his perhaps coming back again. But he had seen the house, seen it was deserted. It was unlikely he'd return. And damn it, if he did come, she would face him. She had no fear of his hurting David. That was all that really counted.

They fell back into the old routines, except that Jeff continued to be more considerate and aware of her than he had been in the past. They exchanged visits with Peggy now and then, and if there was still the buried doubt about her and Jeff, nothing happened to aggravate it, to suggest that something was still going on. If anything ever had.

One morning that fall it started to rain. Jeff was at work. The rain began to come down harder and by noon it hadn't slackened. The brook rose, darkened by the silt running into it as water poured down the hills, spilled over from the road.

It didn't worry or frighten her. Instead she found it exciting. She wrapped David up in a small parka, threw one on herself, then took him out, held him in her arms as she strode out onto the small bridge, and faced upstream. The water was very high now, inches from the bridge, sending spouts of water up between the planks.

The water coming toward her, normally clear and lively, had risen into waves, great roiled breakers heaving up over the boulders that stood in the brook, swift-moving, ominous. Very quickly, with David still exclaiming excitedly, she retreated. The water had leapt higher even in these few moments. It was now nearly even with the bridge.

Inside the house she started to take David to his playroom. Halfway in, she stood rooted. Through the windows she could see the brook at the far end of their property. There, where it was, unlike by the house, much closer to ground level, it had risen so high it was beginning to flow across the grass and toward the house.

"Look!" she cried, and showed David. There was nothing frightening about this: the rain had slackened considerably, and the water was only a couple of inches high; it seemed unlikely it would get worse. "Just like the flood in *Winnie-the-Pooh*," she told David, and he nodded happily. He'd been entranced by that chapter in the book.

Suddenly she thought of the lawn furniture on the patio; aluminum chairs that might be swept away even in a flood as mild as this. She told David to stay put, then quickly ran out, gathered the chairs and stacked them on the front porch. The water was nearly three inches high now, but a natural dam of debris had formed against the low bushes that bordered the house, diverting the water, allowing it to flow harmlessly on past the front and back sides.

Five minutes later, when Jeff called, the brook was already beginning to drop. "The cellar is flooded," she told him. "We may need some work on the furnace. But I have to admit it's been exciting."

"I envy you," Jeff told her. "I've always wanted to be in a flood. Well, anyway, one like this. I'll be home as soon as I can."

The furnace did need work, and there was mopping

up to do, but Frances didn't mind. She, too, had always been fascinated by the idea of a flood. More important, her reaction to all of it made her hope that the worst was over; she'd treated it all lightly, enjoyed herself, most of all hadn't worried, hadn't been fearful.

Three days later, she noticed the smell.

It seemed to come from the crawl space under David's playroom. "The water level in the ground's probably still pretty high. Bound to be some puddles down there," Jeff told her. "Just fetid water. Dampness. Nothing to worry about. Should be gone in a day or two."

But it didn't go away.

She mentioned it to Jeff again, but once more he sloughed it off, assured her it would disappear. There was nothing he could do anyway, not just now. He was packing for a trip to Rhode Island. "If it bothers you, just keep David out of the playroom till it goes away. It will, believe me."

But if anything, the odor was even worse the next day, and the following day and the day after that. David was in pre-kindergarten now, and her afternoons were free. She didn't know if she could take the smell any longer. Maybe they'd have to have someone pump out the crawl space. Or maybe somehow something once alive had been swept in there and was rotting . . . She took a flashlight out of her dresser drawer and went outside.

Frances leaned down into the window well that fronted the crawl space and, with some difficulty, pulled the screen out, away from the moisture-swollen frame. Putting the screen down, she switched on the flashlight and, one hand supporting herself, leaned down into the well. The light barely penetrated the murk. If she were going to find anything, she'd have to slip down into the space. She lowered herself feet first into the well, her legs sliding into and past the opening. Slowly she edged the rest of herself down. The smell now was almost overpowering.

Half of her still outside, she hesitated, nearly overcome by the stench. But she forced herself to wriggle the rest of the way into the opening. Then she slowly lowered herself to the dirt floor of the crawl space, stood in a half crouch. Almost immediately she began to gag.

Trying to hold her breath, Frances swept the flashlight across the ground. There were reflections that intimated water, but between them were long dark spaces, suggesting the puddles were small and few. Some of the darkness was in the form of shapes that seemed to rise up from the ground. She tried to remember from the time she'd been down here before. Hadn't everything been level? She fixed the flashlight on one of the mounds and moved toward it.

As she drew closer the light began to pick out details. She fixed the beam on an area just in front of her, tried to pick out what it was. Long, thin, tapering things seemed to be what she saw. Whitish. Like fingers. She edged closer, held the light directly above them. Stared very hard. Ran the beam back and forth over it. Edged to the side, for another angle.

And felt her whole universe sinking. There was no question now.

It *was* a hand. She began to shake and sway. But she forced herself to move the flashlight slowly, trace its light along the form. The hand, and then an arm, and then . . . the body. A portion of a body where it had been pushed up through the ground by the rising waters. There was hair now, too. Long. Flowing almost to her feet. Gasping, she fell back against the concrete wall, ran the flashlight over the rest of the space.

She knew now what she was looking for, was able to immediately recognize what she saw for what it was. A foot. A leg. Breasts. Scattered throughout the confines of the four walls that enclosed her. Staggering, she moved back toward the small opening. As she did, the beam fell on something else. Despite herself she halted for an instant, stared down. She'd recognized it immediately. The water had washed it clean where it had emerged from the earth. There was a dark stain covering part of it. It was Jeff's jacket.

She flung herself toward the opening, unable to take any more. *Jeff*. All along it had been *Jeff*. Killing them, only now bringing them here, burying them. Where they wouldn't be found. The reason why he hadn't sold the house. The reason why he'd tried so hard to dissuade her from coming back.

She flung her arms through the opening, extended her arms to the outer edge of the window well, fingertips slicing open as she desperately pressed her hands against the concrete. All at once Frances halted. Before she raised her eyes, she knew. Inches from her. A pair of highly polished black shoes, cuffs of dark flannel trousers grazing the tops of them. The tops of Jeff's shoes.

Chapter
29

THERE WAS NOTHING SHE COULD DO. SHE COULDN'T RE-
treat. He would follow her in, destroy her there.

Slowly Frances raised herself up, felt his hand suddenly grip her wrist as if it had been welded there.

"You had to meddle," Jeff said. His voice was almost
weary.

They were at the back of the house. Leaves were
falling from the trees, drifting lazily through the fall
air. The brook, nearly back to its normal levels, was
making its accustomed erratic, lightly rushing sounds.
Shadows were beginning to lengthen.

"I'm going to have to kill you now," he told her. His
mouth was a thin line, his eyes without life. "I've always wanted to," he said after a moment. Then he
shook his head. "Well, no. Not always. Sometimes I
hoped that you would save me. That's all I felt at the
beginning, when we first met. It started long before
you, you see. But later, even when I hoped you would
save me, I wanted to do it. To kill you. Came close to
it. More than once."

That night. That terrifying first night, so long ago.

"The kitten. David's kitten," she cried, suddenly understanding.

"Yes. I'd planned to do it that night. Left my car down the road, so you wouldn't hear. Crept up to the house. But I also didn't want to do it, you see. Because I loved you. Because I knew if I did it to you, that would be the time I'd be found out. You were too close. Not a stranger, like the rest. I fought it, hard, but I still came in. And then—just as I came in, there was the kitten. And it came to me that if I killed it, it might be enough. Might get rid of the feelings. Save you. Save me. It worked. I showed it to you so you wouldn't suspect me. The next morning I loosened the wires on the car. *Before* I called the mechanic."

All of it becoming clear, so clear, like a light, shining . . . "The break-in," she breathed.

"To set things up. In case I did kill you. On the chance I would. I didn't know . . . So there would be a diversion—a possible other suspect. I even thought about doing it to you that night. Might have. But . . . on the way back . . . a woman whose car had broken down . . ."

"Why?" she asked him. *"Why?"*

Something in him seemed to crumple. "I don't know," he said. His voice fell to a whisper, became almost childlike. "I don't know. I've never understood. I didn't want to. I've never wanted to. Except . . . those times. Those times when I couldn't do anything about it. Putting on the chains. Making them look like slaves. Like something I owned. Like something I could do anything I wanted to with."

He led her a few steps away, nearer the center of the house, where they couldn't be seen from the road. "The night I gave you the necklace," he continued, "I didn't think I was going to kill you. I really didn't. It was just an amusement. To do to you what I'd done to the others. Stripping you nude, putting on the chain. The idea of it—my doing it, your not knowing—that was enough. I thought that would be enough. Now I don't know. I don't think I was going to do it, but I don't know. I didn't always think I was going to kill the other ones."

"But Alabama . . ." She faltered. "So far away . . . I thought Terrence . . ."

A smile began to play on his lips. "I'd wondered if you'd think that. Yes. Your man wasn't good at covering his tracks. After I got out of the hospital, I tracked him down through his professional association; Peggy had told me what he did. Easy to get into their computer. They had his new workplace. But I couldn't find your damn house. I would have, but I met this woman . . . She was alone, it was dark . . . Then I knew I had to get out of there. For a while. Later, when I went back, you were gone."

This time there was no weapon. Nothing but her fist. She flung it down and then up, up into his crotch. He cried out, his grip loosening, and she tore away.

She began to run. Around the corner of the house, up the driveway, across the road, into the hill on the other side, the thickly forested hill. Within moments she could hear him behind her, grunting, breaking through the underbrush. Lungs burning, she angled toward her left, urged her body on, drove her legs into the ground, oblivious to the branches that tore at her face . . .

She heard him stumble, then crash to the ground, heard him swearing, cursing her, scrambling to his feet, heard the small explosions of the brush behind her, cracking and snapping as he hurtled through it.

Her lungs were on fire, her entire body a mass of agony. Everything in her strained for her to scream, to cry out in her desperation for help, but there was no one to hear her, no breath to spare.

She was near the top of the hill now, saw Mrs. Emenesky's house rising up before her. The labored breathing behind her, the gasps, seemed closer now.

Desperately she threw herself forward, limbs flying out awkwardly, eyes burning. She neared the house, rounded it, came to the front door, prayed it wasn't locked.

She fell forward against it as her hand twisted frantically at the handle. It flew open. She was inside. Even as she pushed the door back behind her, locked it, he threw himself against it.

Screaming, screaming with the utter despair born of a nightmare, she fled from the door into the depths of the house. All at once an inner door flew open. Mrs. Emenesky rushing out of the kitchen, a glint of light, the shattering sound of the door behind her. And then a noise that seemed to explode into eternity, an explosion so mighty that it surpassed sound, became an unending explosion of silence. And then, all at once, there was blackness.

Chapter
30

"SHE KEPT SAYING, 'MY HUSBAND'S RIFLE, MY HUSBAND'S rifle,'" Frances murmured. "As if it was an explanation. An apology."

They were at Peggy's. David was asleep. The police had gone. Finally even the television cameras and the microphones had left. "I know," Peggy said. "She was still pretty shaken up when I saw her. Even though she'd done the right thing. Destroyed that monster."

She took Frances' hand, pressed her other hand over it. "You know there was nothing between Jeff and me. Never was."

Frances tried to demur, but Peggy went on. "It's okay. I saw your looks. I could see why you'd wonder. It hurt me a little, but with all that happened to you . . . Jesus, kid, I don't blame you for a second. Never did."

Frances embraced Peggy, held her fast. "Thank you. Thank you for everything."

"For being a sister. That's all it amounts to," Peggy told her softly. "Hey, but that's all that counts, isn't it kid?" Then she snapped "Damn," as the phone rang.

"Let it ring. It's probably just another reporter."

Peggy shook her head. "No. It might wake David. Besides, if I don't get rid of them now, they'll just call again." She went to the phone, picked it up. She listened for a moment, and then she held the phone out to Frances. There was a peculiar expression on her face. "It's for you," she said.

Uncertainly, Frances rose and took the phone from Peggy. It took her a full moment to put it to her ear. "Hello?" she said.

The voice at the other end was very low, and tender. "I've found you," it told her. It was Terrence.

Carole Jensen, secure in the love of her handsome husband and the company of her sophisticated friends, takes her charmed life in a quiet suburban town for granted—until it's all destroyed by a vicious rape.

As painful as the attack was physically, far more wounding are the questions Carole finds herself asking of everyone she loves—because the rapist knew her name.

With the help of an ex-New York cop, Carole struggles to restore her shaken faith in humanity. But as a manhunt is begun to track down her attacker, Carole, pushed to the limits of fury and obsessed with revenge, will exact her own form of justice...

ACT of RAGE

A novel of gripping suspense by

JOSEPH HAYES

PETER JAMES

INTERNATIONALLY BESTSELLING AUTHOR OF
POSSESSION

DREAMER

What's a beautiful, happy, successful woman to think of her dreams? Samantha Curtis lives in fear of her childhood nightmare, the one she had just before awakening to learn of her parents' deaths. And now she dreams again, of a mysterious hooded man, of tragic disasters and heinous crimes—that begin to spill over into reality. And as she watches her perfect life drift over the edge of sanity, Sam scrambles in search of answers, a mere heartbeat ahead of her bizarre vision portraying her own terrible death....

SHATTERED

*...by a mindless act of violence that changed his life forever,
James Dewitt decided to become a cop.*

SHACKLED

*...by a web of red tape and corruption, Dewitt now fights
desperately to solve a string of murders cleverly
staged to look like suicides.*

SUBMERGED

*...in the deranged world of the psychopathic mind, Dewitt
struggles to outwit the killer—before it's too late...*

Pr•bable
CAUSE

RIDLEY PEARSON

"FASCINATING...BREATHLESS!"—Chicago Tribune

LANDMARK BESTSELLERS FROM ST. MARTIN'S PAPERBACKS

THE SILENCE OF THE LAMBS
Thomas Harris
_____ 92458-5 $5.99 U.S./$6.99 Can.

SEPTEMBER
Rosamunde Pilcher
_____ 92480-1 $5.99 U.S./$6.99 Can.

BY WAY OF DECEPTION
Victor Ostrovsky and Claire Hoy
_____ 92614-6 $5.99 U.S.

LAZARUS
Morris West
_____ 92460-7 $5.95 U.S./$6.95 Can.

THE GULF
David Poyer
_____ 92577-8 $5.95 U.S./$6.95 Can.

MODERN WOMEN
Ruth Harris
_____ 92272-8 $5.95 U.S./$6.95 Can.